37664

This book is to be returned on or before
the last date stamped below. P1-3

READING
COLLECTION

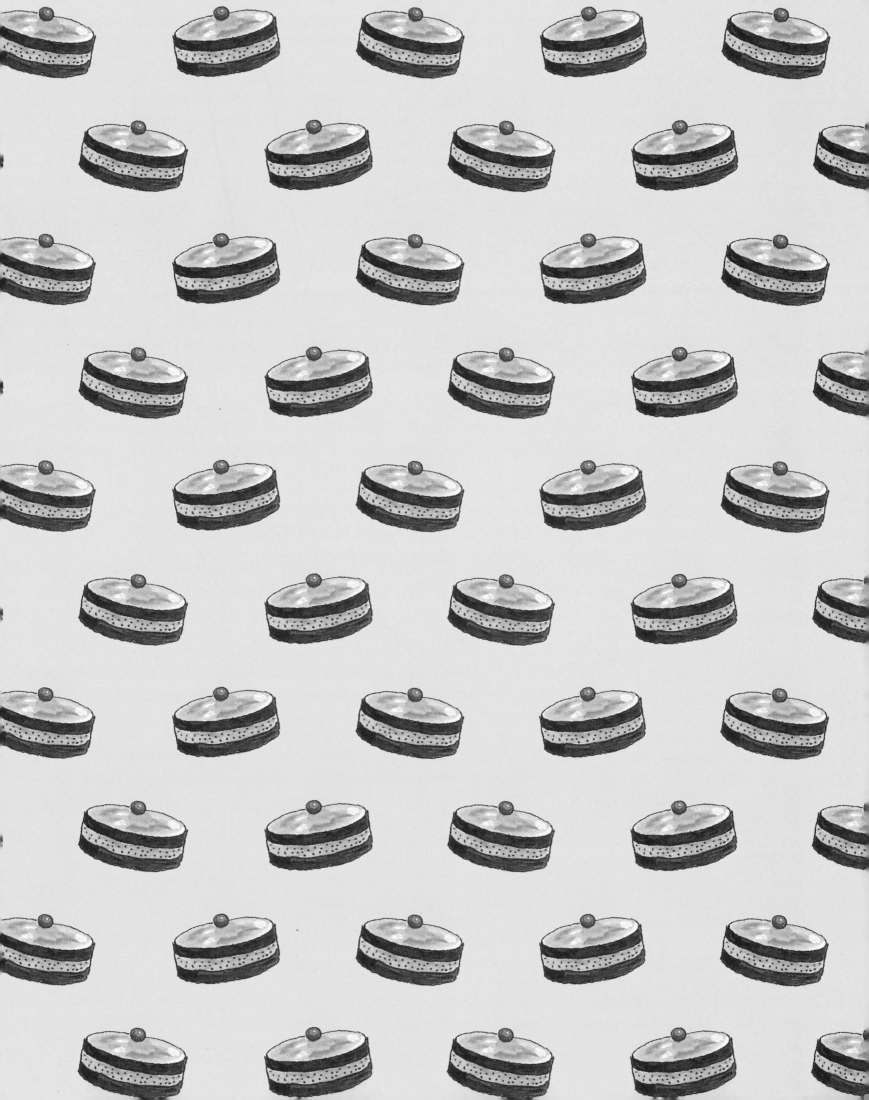

Illustrations copyright © 2004, Thé Tjong-Khing

Original edition © 2004, Uitgeverij Lannoo nv, Tielt, www.lannoo.com

Original title: *Waar is de Taart?* Translated from the Dutch language

English translation © 2007, Harry N. Abrams, Inc.

Library of Congress Control Number for the first English edition of this book: 2006926330
Paperback ISBN 978-0-8109-8924-5

Printed and bound in China
10 9 8 7 6 5 4 3 2 1

Abrams Books for Young Readers are available at special discounts when purchased in quantity
for premiums and promotions as well as fundraising or educational use. Special editions can also be created
to specification. For details, contact specialmarkets@abramsbooks.com or the address below.

ABRAMS
THE ART OF BOOKS SINCE 1949

The Market Building
72-82 Rosebery Avenue
London
EC1R 4RW
www.abramsbooks.co.uk

Where Is the Cake?

T. T. Khing

Abrams Books for Young Readers
New York

the architect, with the employer's consent, can let errors remain and can reduce the Contract Sum instead.

8 MATERIALS, GOODS AND WORKMANSHIP, including performance specified work, must conform to the standards referred to in the Contract Bills or, if required, be to the architect's satisfaction. If no standards are specified in the Bills, the workmanship must be appropriate to the works. The architect may request vouchers from the contractor to prove conformity. Where materials, goods and workmanship are to be to the architect's satisfaction, he or she must express any dissatisfaction within a reasonable time of the execution of the work. All work must be carried out in accordance with the Health and Safety Plan. If the architect requires the opening up of the works for inspection or tests to be carried out, he or she may instruct accordingly, but the cost will be added to the Contract Sum (unless the tests reveal noncompliance with the contract). The architect may issue instructions to have work, goods, etc. which do not conform to the contract removed from site, allow the work to remain (with agreement of employer) and reduce the Contract Sum, require a variation at no extra cost or entitling an extension of time, and (having considered the Code of Practice attached to the Conditions) require opening up of the works for inspection or tests to establish similar noncompliance at no extra cost. Work must be carried out in a workmanlike manner and, in default, the architect may issue necessary instructions at no extra cost or entitling an extension of time. The architect may issue instructions requiring the exclusion of any site worker but not unreasonably or vexatiously.

9 The contractor must indemnify the employer against any liability accruing from infringement of PATENT RIGHTS, and is responsible for the payment of ROYALTIES in connection with the Contract, the sum of which is deemed to be included in the Contract Sum.
   However, if the contractor uses or supplies patented goods etc. in compliance with the architect's instructions, liability for infringement is avoided, and any damages or royalty payments are added to the Contract Sum.

10 The contractor must keep a competent PERSON-IN-CHARGE at the Works at all times. Instructions issued to this person by the architect or directions issued by the clerk of works are deemed to be issued to the contractor.

11 The architect must have ACCESS 'at all reasonable times' to the site and workshops of the contractor, who must secure a similar right to the shops of the nominated sub-contractors and domestic sub-contractors. The right of access is subject to reasonable restrictions by the contractor and any sub-contractor necessary to protect their proprietary interests.

12 The employer may engage a CLERK OF WORKS as site inspector, who may give directions to the contractor only if affecting a matter in which the architect has power to give instructions, and then only if such directions are confirmed in writing within 2 days by the architect, when they become Architect's Instructions.

13 VARIATIONS are defined as:
   • Alterations or modifications to the design, quality or quantity of the work described in the Contract Drawings (including standards, or kind of materials, or goods, or Bills).
   • Addition, alteration, omission or substitution of work, obligations, restrictions imposed by the employer (that is, access to the site, limitations of workspace or working hours and the execution of work in a specific order, but not nominating a sub-contractor to do work set out and priced by the contractor in the Bills for execution.
   • Instructions regarding the expending of provisional sums in the Contract Bills. The architect *may* retrospectively sanction variations made without permission. All variation valuations are generally made by the quantity surveyor, who follows the rules set out in this clause. Valuation of variations may be on the basis of a quotation submitted by the contractor e.g. clause 13A (see page 73). Variations made by the architect for work carried out by a nominated sub-contractor are valued according to provisions in sub-contract NSC/C. A variation (within reasonable time limits) will not vitiate the contract.

14 The quality and quantity of the work specified in the CONTRACT SUM is that detailed in the Contract Bills.

15 VALUE ADDED TAX – SUPPLEMENTAL PROVISIONS refers to the VAT agreement (to be found at the back of the Conditions). The Contract Sum is exclusive of VAT.

16 MATERIALS AND GOODS UNFIXED OR OFF-SITE must not be removed (except for use on site) without the architect's written consent, which should not be withheld unreasonably. Once the value of the goods is included in an Interim Certificate, they become the property of the employer (whether on site or not), but the contractor remains responsible for them, and liable in respect of their loss or damage. Off-site materials, the value of which is to be included within interim payments, are identified in the Contract Bills and called 'listed items'.

17 Provisions for the issuance of certificates of PRACTICAL COMPLETION, DEFECTS LIABILITY and COMPLETION OF MAKING GOOD DEFECTS (see page 86).

18 PARTIAL POSSESSION by the employer of part of the works with the contractor's consent (which must not be unreasonably withheld). The architect must immediately issue a written statement identifying the part and the date it was taken into possession. Possession indicates practical completion of the part and the date of possession governs the Defects Liability Period. The contractor's obligation to insure under 22A ceases for the relevant part and the employer carries the risk from the date of possession. Potential Liquidated Damages are reduced in proportion to the value of the part possessed.

19 The employer and the contractor must not ASSIGN THE CONTRACT without the written consent of the other, but the employer may assign the right to bring proceedings in his or her name to a transferee or lessee of the works after practical completion. The contractor must not SUB-LET any part of the works without the architect's written permission (which should not be withheld unreasonably). Where the work described in the Bills is to be executed by a domestic sub-contractor, selected by the contractor from a list in the Bills, the list must not contain less than three alternatives. Any sub-letting must provide for determination of the sub-contractor's employment should the contractor's employment be determined, for ownership of goods to pass to the employer on payment of the contractor by the employer and that the sub-contract must allow the sub-contractor interest for any failure to pay by the contractor in accordance with the sub-contractor.

20 The contractor must take responsibility for, and INDEMNIFY the employer against:
   • personal injury or death caused by execution of the works except and in so far as caused by the negligence of the employer or those for whom the employer is responsible;
   • injury to property (except the works) caused by execution of the works in so far as due to the

negligence of the contractor or those for whom the contractor is responsible.

21 The contractor must maintain the necessary INSURANCE in respect of injury, death or damage to property and ensure compliance with the Employer's Liability (Compulsory Insurance) Act 1969. The contractor must produce evidence of their existence to the architect for inspection by the employer and, where reasonably and not vexatiously required by the employer, produce the actual policies. In default of the contractor insuring, the employer may insure and then charge the contractor, or deduct the sum from monies due to the latter.

Where so stated in the Appendix, the contractor, if instructed by the architect, must maintain insurance in the joint names of the contractor and the employer for: collapse, subsidence, heave, etc. with certain limited exceptions, such as nuclear risk, contractor's negligence, damage due to omissions or errors in design, foreseeable inevitable damage, etc.

22 INSURANCE OF THE WORKS

22A relates to the erection of a new building where the contractor maintains a joint names policy for all risks insurance.

22B provides for the employer to maintain a joint names policy for all risks insurance.

22C relates to alterations or extensions. The employer must maintain a joint names policy for all risks insurance in respect of the works and a joint names policy for insurance against specified perils in respect of the existing structures and contents.

The irrelevant clauses, therefore, should be struck out.

Where the contractor insures under 22A, the employer must approve the insurers and the premium receipts and policies must be deposited with the latter. In default of the contractor insuring, the employer may insure and then charge the contractor, or deduct the sum from the monies due.

The contractor's obligations under this clause may be discharged if, aside from contractual obligations, an insurance policy is maintained in joint names against all risks, but the employer can demand documentary evidence of such maintenance or require to see the policy (not unreasonably or vexatiously).

Where the employer is to insure under 22B or 22C, the contractor has the right to inspect the premium receipts and policies and, if the employer defaults, may affect the insurance in joint names. On production of the receipts, the

amount is to be added to the Contract Sum. If any loss or damage is occasioned by any insured risk, the contractor must immediately give notice (of the nature, location and extent of the damage) to both the employer and the architect.

Clause 22A states the contractor's obligations for insurance claims.

Under clauses 22B and 22C, restoration of the damaged work etc. is to be treated as a Variation required by an Architect's Instruction. Under clause 22C, the employment of the contractor may be determined by either party (if 'just and equitable') after 28 days, any disputes then to be referred under the dispute procedures of the contract. The contractor need not indemnify the employer, and is not responsible for any injury or damage caused by radiation and other nuclear perils, or to the consequences of pressure from supersonic or sonic aircraft. If so stated in the Appendix, the architect may (under 22D), instruct the contractor to obtain quotations for insurance against loss of liquidated damages due to an extension of time being given by reason of specified perils. If the employer so wishes, the contractor must take out and maintain such insurance and the amounts of premiums will be added to the Contract Sum. If the contractor defaults, the employer may take out the insurance. If stated in the Appendix, the parties must comply with the Joint Fire Code set out in 22FC.

23 On the DATE OF POSSESSION, the site must be given to the contractor, but the employer may defer possession for up to 6 weeks if so stated in the Appendix. The contractor must proceed 'regularly and diligently', completing on or before the COMPLETION DATE. Postponement of work is possible only by an Architect's Instruction. If the employer wishes to use or occupy the site before Practical Completion, insurers must confirm that such use will not prejudice the insurance. The contractor may then give written consent (not to be unreasonably withheld). Any additional premium will be added to the Contract Sum.

24 DAMAGES FOR NON-COMPLETION. If the contractor does not finish on time, the architect must issue a certificate to that effect, after which time the contractor will be liable to pay liquidated and ascertained damages at the rate stated in the Appendix if the employer gives a written notice not later than 5 days before the final date for payment of any debt due under the final certificate. If the architect fixes a later Completion Date, the employer must

repay the damages and the architect must issue a further certificate under this clause.

25 EXTENSIONS OF TIME (see page 80).

26 LOSS AND EXPENSE (to the contractor) CAUSED BY MATTERS MATERIALLY AFFECTING THE REGULAR PROGRESS OF THE WORKS, which are allowed no payment elsewhere under the contract, are ascertained by the architect, or the quantity surveyor on an Instruction by the architect. The claim must be promptly made by the contractor, who should be prepared to show details and proof of the loss, and to supply any other information needed to enable the architect to form an opinion. Possible claims could be made for:
- not receiving information (drawings, instructions etc.) specifically requested in writing from the architect in due time;
- opening up for inspection or testing (unless the work was shown not to be in accordance with the contract);
- discrepancies or divergencies between the contract drawings and the Bills;
- work completed (or not completed) by the employer which forms no part of the contract;
- supply (or non-supply) of materials and/or goods by the employer;
- Architect's Instructions in respect of postponement, variations or expenditure of a provisional sum;
- the employer's failure to give sufficient access (in or out) to the site etc.;
- employer's deferment of possession of the site;
- approximate quantities not a reasonably accurate forecast;
- compliance or non-compliance by the employer with the CDM Regulations;
- rightful suspension by the contractor following employer's failure to pay.

Certain extensions of time have to be notified in writing to the contractor if they affect loss and/or expense ascertainment (26.3). If the contractor receives a claim from a nominated sub-contractor for loss or expense, it must be passed on to the architect for ascertainment. The architect will then send a written statement of the revision of the period of completion to the contractor, with a copy for the nominated sub-contractor. Any amounts ascertained under this clause are added to the Contract Sum.

27 DETERMINATION BY THE EMPLOYER (see page 94)

28 DETERMINATION BY THE CONTRACTOR (see page 94).

28a DETERMINATION BY EMPLOYER OR CONTRACTOR (see page 94).

29 WORKS BY THE EMPLOYER (or employees) which do not form part of the contract, but information on which is provided in the Contract Bills, must be allowed by the contractor. If there is no such information in the Bills, the contractor's consent is required.

30 CERTIFICATES are issued from time to time (specified in the Appendix – monthly unless stated otherwise) by the architect on work that has been valued by the quantity surveyor. There is express provision permitting the contractor to submit an application for payment to the quantity surveyor. (The quantity surveyor is to notify the contractor to the extent that there is disagreement with the contractor's application in the same level of detail as the contractor's application.) This entitles the contractor to payment from the employer within 14 days (the final date for payment) from the date of issue (the due date for payment), less any deduction, for example, the retention sum, which is generally calculated at 5% unless a different rate is agreed. Rules affecting the treatment of the retention are set out in this clause.

Provision exists under the contract for the contractor to receive advance payments which need to be taken into account when calculating the amount due to the contractor.

Within five days of the date of issue of a payment certificate, the employer is to give notice to the contractor of the amount intended for payment, to what the payment relates and the basis on which it was calculated. No later than 5 days before the final date for payment, the employer is to give notice of any amount that will be withheld, including the grounds for withholding and the amounts against each ground if more than one.

Should the employer not pay the amount due, subject to any proper notice to withhold, by the final date for payment, the contractor is entitled to interest.

The architect cannot be required to issue an Interim Certificate less than 1 month after the previous certificate was issued. Off-site materials and goods ('listed items') may be included in the valuation at the discretion of the architect and on certain conditions (that the goods or materials are finished, insured, clearly marked, and that proof can be shown of ownership and destination). A draft bond to protect the employer when paying for off-site materials or goods can be made a requirement under the contract).

Not later than 6 months after Practical Completion, the contractor must submit all necessary documents for the final adjustment of the Contract Sum. Within 3 months thereafter, the quantity surveyor must complete any ascertainment of loss and/or expense, prepare the final adjustment of the Contract Sum, and send details to the contractor. The items to be included in the adjustment are set out in this clause (30.6). As soon as practical (but not less than 28 days prior to the issue of the Final Certificate), the architect must issue an interim certificate showing the final adjustment of nominated sub-contractor sums. The Final Certificate is issued before two months have expired from the later of the end of the Defects Liability period, the issue of Making Good of Defects Certificate or sending of the adjustment statement to the contractor. The Final Certificate must be honoured within 28 days (the final date for payment) and is conclusive (subject to no adjudication, arbitration or other proceedings having been commenced) that:

- work is to the architect's reasonable satisfaction if expressly so required;
- all the financial provisions of the contract have been observed;
- all due extensions of time have been given;
- reimbursement under clause 26.1 is in final settlement of all claims arising out of clause 26.2 for breach of contract or in tort.

The same notices (e.g. withholding notice and notice periods) apply to the final certificate as to interim certificates.

31 INCOME AND CORPORATION TAXES ACT 1988 – STATUTORY TAX DEDUCTION SCHEME. This only applies to persons who are 'contractors' and 'sub-contractors' for purposes of the Act, ensuring that the contractor tells employers whether or not statutory deductions are to be made, and giving proof of reasons for non-deductions if necessary. If deductions are to be made, the contractor must inform the employer and send the architect a copy.

34 ANTIQUITIES, upon discovery, become the property of the employer, and the contractor must try to protect and preserve any findings, informing the architect (or clerk of works), who will issue instructions on the matter. If these result in direct loss or expense to the contractor, the architect may ascertain the amount and add it to the Contract Sum (an extension of time may also be allowed).

Part Two: Nominated sub-contractors and nominated suppliers

(see page 64).

Part Three: Fluctuations

Part Four: Settlement of disputes – Adjudication – Arbitration – Legal Proceedings

(see page 96)

Part Five: Performance specified work

42 Under this provision, the contractor undertakes to design parts of the works. This part needs to be identified in the Appendix and the performance requirements clearly identified in the contract documents or as a provisional sum. The architect remains responsible for the integration of the performance specified works.

Appendix

containing dates, figures, rates, rules, time allowances etc.

Supplemental provisions

(the VAT agreement)

References

JCT Standard Form of Building Contract 1998 Edition, Private with Quantities.
ARCHITECT'S LEGAL HANDBOOK, pp. 59–161.

Appendix

Clause etc.	Subject	
Fourth recital and 31	Statutory tax deduction scheme	Employer at Base Date *is a 'contractor'/is not a 'contractor' for the purposes of the Act and the Regulations
Fifth recital	CDM Regulations	*All the CDM Regulations apply/ Regulations 7 and 13 only of the CDM Regulations apply
Articles 7A and 7B 41B 41C	Dispute or difference – settlement of disputes	*Clause 41B applies *Delete if disputes are to be decided by legal proceedings and article 7B is thus to apply *See the Guidance Note to JCT 80 Amendment 18 on factors to be taken into account by the Parties considering whether disputes are to be decided by arbitration or by legal proceedings*
1·3	Base Date	29 January 2002
1·3	Date for Completion	17 December 2002
1·11	Electronic data interchange	The JCT Supplemental Provisions for EDI *apply/do not apply If applicable: the EDI Agreement to which the Supplemental Provisions refer is: *the EDI Association Standard EDI Agreement *the European Model EDI Agreement
15·2	VAT Agreement	Clause 1A of the VAT Agreement *applies/does not apply [x]
17·2	Defects Liability Period (if none other stated is 6 months from the day named in the certificate of Practical Completion of the Works)	6 Months
19·1·2	Assignment by Employer of benefits after Practical Completion	Clause 19·1·2 *applies/does not apply
21·1·1	Insurance cover for any one occurrence or series of occurrences arising out of one event	£ 2,000,000

Clause etc.	Subject	
21·2·1	Insurance – liability of Employer	Insurance *may be required/is not required Amount of indemnity for any one occurrence or series of occurrences arising out of one event £ 500,000 [aaa]
22·1	Insurance of the Works – alternative clauses	*Clause 22A/Clause 22B/Clause 22C applies (See footnote [cc] to clause 22) 10%
*22A, 22B·1, 22C·2	Percentage to cover professional fees	
22A·3·1	Annual renewal date of insurance as supplied by Contractor	Not Applicable
22D	Insurance for Employer's loss of liquidated damages – clause 25·4·3	Insurance *may be required/is not required
22D·2		Period of time
22FC·1	Joint Fire Code	The Joint Fire Code *applies/does not apply If the Joint Fire Code is applicable, state whether the insurer under clause 22A or clause 22B or clause 22C·2 has specified that the Works are a 'Large Project': *YES/NO (where clause 22A applies these entries are made on information supplied by the Contractor)
23·1·1	Date of Possession	30 January 2002
23·1·2, 25·4·13, 26·1	Deferment of the Date of Possession	Clause 23·1·2 *applies/does not apply Period of deferment if it is to be less than 6 weeks is 4 weeks
24·2	Liquidated and ascertained damages	at the rate of £ 250-00 per week
28·2·2	Period of suspension (if none stated is 1 month)	One month
28A·1·1·1 to 28A·1·1·3	Period of suspension (if none stated is 3 months)	Three months
28A·1·1·4 to 28A·1·1·6	Period of suspension (if none stated is 1 month)	One month

Footnotes

*Delete as applicable.

[x] Clause 1A can only apply where the Contractor is satisfied at the date the Contract is entered into that his output tax on all supplies to the Employer under the Contract will be at either a positive or a zero rate of tax.

On and from 1 April 1989 the supply in respect of a building designed for a 'relevant charitable purpose' (as defined in the legislation which gives statutory effect to the VAT changes operative from 1 April 1989) is only zero rated if the person to whom the supply is made has given to the Contractor a certificate in statutory form: see the VAT leaflet 708 revised 1989. Where a contract supply is zero rated by certificate only the person holding the certificate (usually the Contractor) may zero rate his supply.

This footnote repeats footnote [x] for clause 15·2.

Footnotes

*Delete as applicable.

[aaa] If the indemnity is to be for an aggregate amount and not for any one occurrence or series of occurrences the entry should make this clear.

Clause etc.	Subject	
30·1·1·6	Advance payment	Clause 30·1·1·6 ~~applies~~/does not apply If applicable: the advance payment will be **£ _____ / _____ % of the Contract Sum and will be paid to the Contractor on _____ and will be reimbursed to the Employer in the following amount(s) and at the following time(s) _____ _____ An advance payment bond *is/is not required
30·1·3	Period of Interim Certificates (if none stated is 1 month)	*One Month*
30·2·1·1	Gross valuation	A priced Activity Schedule ~~is~~/is not attached to this Appendix
30·3·1	Listed items – uniquely identified	*For uniquely identified listed items a bond as referred to in clause 30·3·1 in respect of payment for such items is required for £ *10,000—00* *Delete if no bond is required
30·3·2	Listed items – not uniquely identified	*For listed items that are not uniquely identified a bond as referred to in clause 30·3·2 in respect of payment for such items is required for £ _____ *Delete if clause 30·3·2 does not apply *5%*
30·4·1·1	Retention Percentage (if less than 5 per cent) [bbb]	*None*
35·2	Work reserved for Nominated Sub-Contractors for which the Contractor desires to tender	
37	Fluctuations: (if alternative required is not shown clause 38 shall apply)	clause 38 [ccc] ~~clause 39~~ ~~clause 40~~

Clause etc.	Subject	
38·7 or 39·8	Percentage addition	*X*%
40·1·1·1	Formula Rules	*NOT Applicable* rule 3: Base Month _____ 19 ___ rules 10 and 30 (i): Part I/Part II [ddd] of Section 2 of the Formula Rules is to apply
41A·2	Adjudication – nominator of Adjudicator (if no nominator is selected the nominator shall be the President or a Vice-President of the Royal Institute of British Architects)	President or a Vice-President or Chairman or a Vice-Chairman: *Royal Institute of British Architects ~~*Royal Institution of Chartered Surveyors~~ ~~*Construction Confederation~~ ~~*National Specialist Contractors Council~~ *Delete all but one
41B·1	Arbitration – appointor of Arbitrator (if no appointor is selected the appointor shall be the President or a Vice-President of the Royal Institute of British Architects)	President or a Vice-President: ~~*Royal Institute of British Architects~~ ~~*Royal Institution of Chartered Surveyors~~ *Chartered Institute of Arbitrators *Delete all but one
42·1·1	Performance Specified Work	Identify below or on a separate sheet each item of Performance Specified Work to be provided by the Contractor and insert the relevant reference in the Contract Bills [zz]

Footnotes

*Delete as applicable.

**Insert either a money amount or a percentage figure and delete the other alternative.

[bbb] The percentage will be 5 per cent unless a lower rate is specified here.

[ccc] Delete alternatives not used.

92

P With 98

Footnotes

[ddd] Strike out according to which method of formula adjustment (Part I – Work Category Method or Part II – Work Group Method) has been stated in the documents issued to tenderers.

[zz] See Practice Note 25 'Performance Specified Work' paragraphs 2·6 to 2·8 for a description of work which is **not** to be treated as Performance Specified Work.

* This footnote repeats footnote [zz] for clause 42.

P With 98

93

59

Tender Action 1

Tendering

At certain points in the design process, it is necessary to consider the appointment of a suitable contractor to undertake the building work. The choice may be made:

- by negotiation
- by competition

Negotiation

This follows the procedure laid out in 'The Code of Procedure for Two Stage Selective Tendering 1996'.

Negotiated contracts

In certain circumstances, it may be advantageous to bring the contractor into the project on a non-competitive basis:

- Where time for construction is limited.
- Where specialised building techniques are involved which can only be undertaken by certain contractors.
- Where the contractor's expertise in a particular situation would be valuable.
- Where the contractor has an established working relationship with the employer.
- Where the project involves additional work to a site where there is an ongoing contract with a contractor.

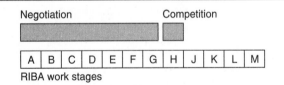

Negotiation   Competition

| A | B | C | D | E | F | G | H | J | K | L | M |
RIBA work stages

A shortlist of suitable contractors can be drawn up, or a specific contractor approached. It is necessary to establish a basis for a negotiated contract, which could be:

- a schedule of prices;
- a priced bill of approximate quantities;
- a priced bill of a recently completed project undertaken by the contractor.

When terms have been negotiated, the employer may send the contractor a LETTER OF INTENT, but only after having received specialist advice. It is better, if possible, to enter into a formal contract at this stage, because letters of intent can have unforeseen consequences.

Competition

Selective or competitive tendering

This allows the procedure laid out in 'The Code of Procedure for Single Stage Selective Tendering 1996' or, if appropriate, 'The Code of Procedure for Selective Tendering for Design and Build 1996'.

1. The shortlist

Selection of a shortlist from:

- client's approved list
- personal experience
- research or recommendation

Based upon the firm's:

- experience and reputation
- financial status
- suitability for the project
- current availability

Checked by:

- questionnaire
- references
- proof of financial status
- inspection of previous or present work
- visit to workshops
- interview

The number on the shortlist should be no more than six, although two reserve names should be appended to the list.

2. Preliminary enquiry

Issuance of the PRELIMINARY ENQUIRY FOR INVITATION TO TENDER.

This should give details of:

- the project and its location;
- the parties involved (including nominated sub-contractors);
- approximate cost range;
- type of contract to be used (and whether as a deed or under hand);
- time stipulations (commencement, completion etc.);
- date of tender document dispatch;
- tender period;
- liquidated damages;
- bond requirements;
- correction of priced bills;
- further conditions, if any.

It is usual to allow 4 to 6 weeks before issuing tender documents. If during this time a firm agrees to participate in tendering procedures, the agreement should be honoured or, if necessary, revoked not later than 2 days after the issuance of the tender documents.

3. Invitation to tender

When the final time for acceptance has passed, a final shortlist of contractors is drawn up, and the unsuccessful parties notified. The contractors placed on the shortlist are then issued:

- a formal invitation to tender;
- a form of tender (2 copies);
- the necessary drawings;
- bill(s) of quantities (2 copies) or, where none, a specification;
- addressed envelopes for the returned tenders;
- addressed envelope for the return of the drawings etc.;
- instructions regarding drawing inspection and site inspection;
- a covering letter.

The employer and the quantity surveyor should also be sent copies of the letter and specification, if used.

Formal invitation to tender

Dear

re: New development at ....

Following your acceptance of the invitation to tender for the above, we now have pleasure in enclosing the following:

A. Two copies of the bills of quantities.
B. Two copies of the general arrangement drawings indicating the general character, shape and disposition of the works.
C. Two copies of the form of tender.
D. Addressed envelopes for the r.turn of the tender and instructions relating thereto.

Will you please also note:
1. Drawings and details may be inspected at ....
2. The site may be inspected by arrangement with ourselves.
3. Tendering procedure will be in accordance with the principles of the 'Code of Procedure for Single Stage Selective Tendering 1996'.
4. Examination and adjustment of priced bills (Section 6 of the Code), Alternative 1/2 (delete as appropriate) will apply.

The completed form of tender is to be sealed in the endorsed envelope provided and delivered or sent by post to reach this office not later than .....hours on ..... the ..... day of ..... 20...

Will you please acknowledge receipt of this letter and enclosures and confirm that you are able to submit a tender in accordance with these instructions.

Yours faithfully

....

Architect/Quantity Surveyor

Form of Tender

This form of tender is used only when a formal contract is entered into.

TENDER FOR _____

TO _____

Dear

We having read the conditions of contract and bills of quantities delivered to us and having examined the drawings referred to therein do hereby offer to execute and complete in accordance with the conditions of contract the whole of the works described for the sum of £........ and within ...... weeks from the date of possession (note: this last insert will be filled in before the Form is sent).

We agree that should obvious errors in pricing or errors in arithmetic be discovered before acceptance of this offer in the priced bills of quantities submitted by us these errors will be dealt with in accordance with Alternative 1/2 (delete as appropriate) contained in Section 6 of the 'Code of Procedure for Single Stage Selective Tendering 1996'.

This tender remains open for consideration for ..... days (note: not normally more than 28 days) from the date fixed for the submission or lodgement of tenders.

Dated this ..... day of .... 20....

Name ....

Address ....

Signature ....

4. Time allowed

The time allowed for tendering depends upon the size and complexity of the project, but should not be less than 4 weeks. If any problems or discrepancies are found in the tender documents, the architect should be notified not less than 10 days before the opening, so that an extension may be granted if the documents need to be amended.

5. The opening

Tenders are opened on the specified date, and any later entries should be promptly returned unopened. Although it is usual for the lowest bid to be accepted, the employer is not bound to follow this. All unsuccessful parties should be promptly notified except for the next two lowest bids (who are informed of their position) and the lowest (generally) who should be asked to submit priced bills of quantities within 4 working days for the quality surveyor to check for errors.

Errors

Errors may be dealt with in two ways:
- ALTERNATIVE 1, where the tenderer may withdraw the offer, or confirm and agree to an endorsement of the bills.
- ALTERNATIVE 2, where the tenderer is allowed to correct genuine errors. However, if the correction causes the base bid to rise above the next lowest bid, the latter will then be examined. If the original tenderer opts not to amend the offer, an endorsement may also be used in this alternative.

In the event that the lowest tenderer exceeds the budget available, negotiations may be entered into by the parties with a view to making reductions.

Once the contract is let, all the tenderers should be sent a list of the comparative tender prices. Care should be taken to ensure all drawings and bills have been returned.

Prior to building commencement, there is a recommended period of detailed project planning and organisation. However, although very important, this period should not be unnecessarily long, as extra costs could be incurred as a result of the delay.

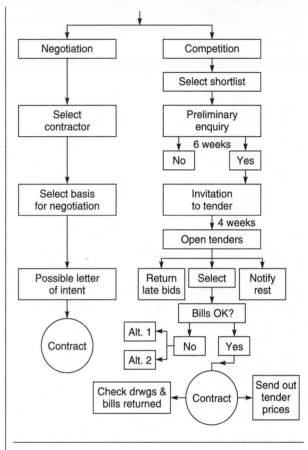

Serial Tenders

These are used for successive phases of the same project or for work involving standardised designs, where the contractor agrees to enter into a series of lump sum contracts.

References

ARCHITECT'S HANDBOOK OF PRACTICE MANAGEMENT, pp. 192–4.
THE ARCHITECT'S GUIDE TO RUNNING A JOB, pp. 70–3, 82–103.
THE ARCHITECT IN PRACTICE, pp. 235–47.

Contract Formation 1

The documents

The contract documents consist of:

No quantities
- form of tender
- drawings
- specification or schedules of work (if any)

With quantities
- form of tender
- drawings
- priced bills of quantities
- relevant standard form

A copy of the standard form and 2 copies of the bills and drawings, with copies of all relevant consents, notices, licences and building notice cards and top copies of sub-contractor's estimates, are sent (preferably by special delivery) to the contractor with a covering letter.

Covering letter

The COVERING LETTER might contain:
- the name of the architect and how he or she can be contacted;
- the name of the clerk of works (if any);
- instructions on the procedure if queries arise;
- names of any relevant local government officials;
- instructions on site possession (including details of the rights of adjoining owners);
- requirement that a contractor's programme be supplied;
- request for details of relevant insurance policies and premium receipts.

Other matters which require attention at contract formation include:
- details of site meetings, including the date of the first site meeting (see page 72);
- provisions for contractor/sub-contractor meetings;
- details of site huts etc.;
- pre-orders for materials;
- procedures for exchange of information;
- signboards, security, etc.

NOTE: if the site is formally handed over to the contractor at commencement of the contract, immediate problems or queries can be dealt with at the same time.

The programme

The master programme is referred to in Clause 5 of the contract (see page 54). The Contract Bills or specification should state the type of programme required.

Gantt (or bar) chart

The individual bars represent specific work areas, while their lengths indicate periods of time involved. This is the simplest type of programme, easily understood and favoured by many site personnel. The bar chart is suitable for simple jobs, is easy to monitor in terms of progress, but does not reflect the reasons for delays very easily.

Network analysis

Activities are represented by arrows converging to, and diverging from, EVENT points. Times are indicated by figures, and the programme is suitable for all types of projects. More complex work may require a computer to update and monitor progress. The CRITICAL PATH and float can be readily determined, and actual and potential delays identified.

Precedence diagram

This is similar in principle to NETWORK ANALYSIS. Activities are shown in boxes together with duration times and float, so that the CRITICAL PATH can be determined. It is relatively easy to understand, and is capable of containing a considerable amount of useful information.

Line of balance

This is only suitable for projects containing a number of similar units (e.g. housing). The chart has three points of reference:
- units
- specific work areas
- time

It is useful for providing an overview of a scheme, but is not easy to update or to record progress.

Use of computers

It is now usual for even relatively small projects to be programmed using sophisticated network or precedence techniques.

There are several excellent software packages which simplify the construction of such a network and permit the information to be plotted in optional program formats.

Once the program is in the computer, the task of updating and of predicting the results of delays or accelerations is simplified. These techniques are widely used by or on behalf of contractors when submitting claims and by architects in estimating extensions of time or assessing the validity of the contractor's assertions. The computer will still produce a simple bar chart for use on site alongside highly detailed delineations of critical paths and earliest and latest start and finish dates.

Gantt (or bar) chart

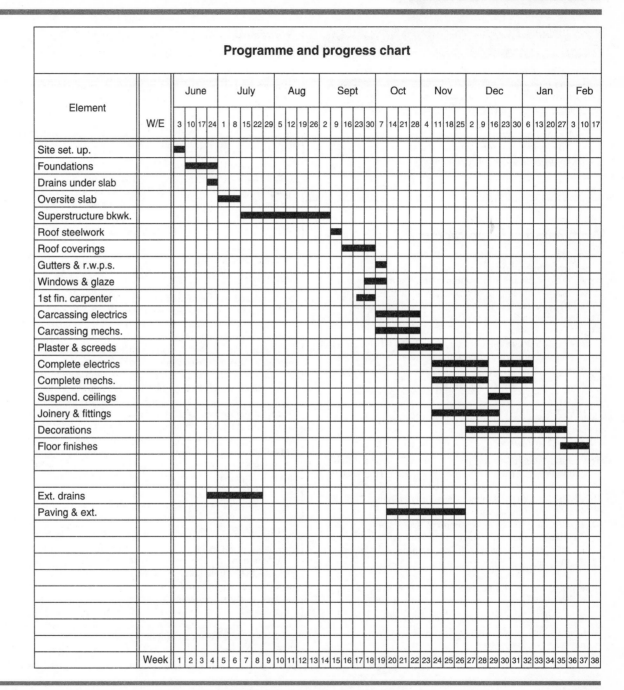

Sub-Contractors/Suppliers

Sub-contractors

On many projects, it is unlikely that the contractor will carry out all the work required by the contract. Parts of the work, particularly those needing specialist attention, may be assigned or sub-let to sub-contractors. These may be:
- domestic sub-contractors, who are employed directly by the contractor;
- nominated sub-contractors, who are proposed by the employer, usually on the architect's advice.

Nominated sub-contractors

A nominated sub-contractor may be selected:
- by inclusion in the Contract Bills;
- in an Architect's Instruction requiring a variation;
- in the expenditure of a provisional sum;
- by agreement with the employer and contractor.

The contractor may make reasonable objection to the choice of sub-contractor, and may also bid for the work. If successful, however, the contractor may not sub-let the work to a domestic sub-contractor without the architect's permission.

Forms of agreement

The 1998 Standard Form, Clause 35.6 to 35.9, lays down procedural rules for the method of nomination (the 1991 procedure). The following forms are used:
- NSC/T – JCT Standard Form of Nominated Sub-contract Tender 1998 Edition.
- NSC/A – JCT Standard Form of Articles of Nominated Sub-contract Agreement 1998 Edition.
- NSC/C – JCT Standard Conditions of Nominated Sub-contract 1998 Edition incorporated by reference into NSC/A.
- NSC/W – JCT Standard Form of Employer/Nominated Sub-contractor Agreement 1998 Edition.
- NSC/N – JCT Standard Form of Nomination Instruction.

Nomination

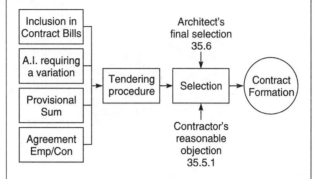

Payment

Upon issuing each interim certificate, the architect directs the contractor as to the amount due to the nominated sub-contractor. The architect must then inform the nominated sub-contractor of the amount payable. Before the issue of the next certificate, the architect must be satisfied that the nominated sub-contractor has been paid. If the contractor does not provide proof, the architect must issue a certificate to that effect which enables the employer to pay the nominated sub-contract direct and to deduct the sum from payment otherwise due to the contractor. When there are two or more nominated sub-contractors and the amount owed to the contractor is not sufficient to pay them in full, the amount available should be applied *pro rata* to all nominated sub-contractors, or some other method which the employer believes to be fair should be adopted, but not if the contractor becomes insolvent.

Extensions

Extension to the nominated sub-contract time limits can only be effected in conformance with the sub-contract. NSC/C requires the written consent of the architect to such an extension. If the nominated sub-contractor fails to complete on time and the contractor informs the architect, the latter must issue a certificate to that effect (within 2 months of notification) if he or she is satisfied that the extension of time provisions have been carried out.

Final payment

Clauses 35.17 to 35.19 of the 1980 Standard Form regulate the final payment of nominated sub-contractors in accordance with various standard forms. In particular, these clauses deal with the procedure where defects are found to exist in the nominated sub-contractor's work after final payment.

Nominated suppliers

Nominated suppliers are proposed by the architect to supply goods or materials fixed by the contractor.
- where a prime cost sum is included in the bills, and the supplier is either named in the bills, or later identified in an Architect's Instruction;
- where a provisional sum is included in the bills which is made the subject of a prime cost sum by an Architect's Instruction in which the supplier is named;
- where there is a provisional sum in the bills and goods for which there is a sole source of supply are specified by the architect in an Architect's Instruction;
- where goods for which there is a sole supplier are specified by the architect in an Architect's Instruction requiring a variation.

In the last two instances, the architect must specify a prime cost sum.

Clause 36 lays down provisions which should exist in the Contract of Sale between the contractor and the nominated supplier, e.g. payment to nominated suppliers is made by the contractor, who is allowed a 5% cash discount if payment is made within 30 days of the end of the month in which the deliveries were made.

If the contractor is out of the pocket as a result of obtaining goods from nominated suppliers, the contractor's expenses are added to the Contract Sum.

References

ARCHITECT IN PRACTICE, pp. 6–7, 271.
THE ARCHITECT'S GUIDE TO RUNNING A JOB, pp. 67, 70–3.

Nomination procedure

- The architect sends the completed NSC/T Part 1 to the prospective sub-contractor together with a blank Part 2, the numbered tender documents and the Appendix to the main contract as it is envisaged to be completed. In addition, the architect must include a copy of NSC/W with the contract details completed.
- The sub-contractor must complete NSC/W and Part 2 of NSC/T and return them to the architect.
- The employer signs Part 2 as approved and enters into NSC/W.
- The architect then sends to the contractor a nomination instruction, NSC/N, plus NSC/T Parts 1 and 2, the numbered tender documents and NSC/W. At the same time the architect must send to the sub-contractor a copy of NSC/W, the completed NSC/W and the main contract Appendix as actually completed.
- The contractor and sub-contractor are to agree the Particular Conditions (NSC/T Part 3) and to enter into a sub-contract on NSC/A within 10 working days of receipt of NSC/N and to send the architect a copy of the completed NSC/A. If the contractor fails to enter into NSC/A the architect must be told either:
  - the date completion of NSC/A is expected, and the architect can fix such date as seems reasonable; or
  - that the failure is due to other matters and the architect may either issue instructions to allow completion; or cancel nomination and omit the work; or if the architect does not consider the matters justify the failure, notify the contractor who must enter into the contract accordingly.

Notes on completion by the Sub-Contractor

NSC/T Part 2

Part 2 – Tender by a Sub-Contractor

To the Employer and Main Contractor

[a] Insert the same details as in NSC/T Part 1, pages 2 and 3.

[a] Main Contract Works and location:
NEW DETACHED HOUSE
1 LETSBY AVENUE, CRINGING, WILTS

In NSC/T Part 2 the expression 'Contract Administrator' is applicable where the Nomination Instruction on Nomination NSC/N will be issued under a Local Authorities version of the Standard Form of Building Contract and by a person who is not entitled to the use of the name 'Architect' under and in accordance with the Architects Act 1997. If so, the expression 'Architect' shall be deemed to have been deleted throughout Tender NSC/T. Where the person who will issue the aforesaid Nomination Instruction is entitled to the use of the name 'Architect' the expression 'Contract Administrator' shall be deemed to have been deleted throughout Tender NSC/T.

[a] Job reference: 8072

[a] Sub-Contract Works:

SWIMMING POOL

In response to the **INVITATION IN NSC/T PART 1**

We WESMEY-SHOVELGON LTD

of (address) 2, THE BARRICADES, CRINGING, WILTS

Tel. No: (0201) 00001

having duly noted the information therein contained or referred to now, upon and subject to the Stipulations on page 8, OFFER for approval by or on behalf of the Employer and acceptance by the Contractor:

to carry out and complete, as a Nominated Sub-Contractor, as part of the Main Contract Works referred to in NSC/T Part 1, the Sub-Contract Works identified in the numbered tender documents listed in NSC/T Part 1 and **in accordance with all the entries we have made in this Tender (subject to agreement on items 1 to 3 with the Main Contractor when we agree the items set out in NSC/T Part 3)** and

*~~in the attached further documents and~~

to complete in agreement with the Main Contractor NSC/T Part 3 (Particular Conditions), to have NSC/T Part 3 signed by us or on our behalf and to execute Agreement NSC/A (Articles of Nominated Sub-Contract Agreement) with the Main Contractor forthwith after receipt of a copy of the Nomination Instruction (Nomination NSC/N) issued to the Main Contractor under clause 35·6 of the Main Contract Conditions,

for the **VAT-exclusive Sub-Contract Sum/VAT-exclusive Tender Sum** (whichever is required by the Invitation to tender, NSC/T Part 1, page 2) of

(words) SIX THOUSAND FOUR HUNDRED AND TWENTY SEVEN POUNDS

£ 6,427.00

*delete if not applicable   (11/98)   **Page 2**

JCT Standard Form of Employer/Nominated Sub-Contractor Agreement

Agreement between a Sub-Contractor prior to being nominated for Sub-Contract Works in accordance with clauses 35·3 to 35·9 of the Standard Form of Building Contract, 1998 Edition, and an Employer

[a] Insert the same details as in NSC/T Part 1, pages 2 and 3.

[a] Main Contract Works ('Works') and location:

NEW DETACHED HOUSE
1, LETSBY AVENUE, CRINGING, WILTS

[a] Job reference: 8072

[a] Sub-Contract Works:

SWIMMING POOL

[b] This Agreement must be executed before the Architect/the Contract Administrator can nominate the Sub-Contractor.

[b] ## This Agreement

made the   15th   day of   JULY   20 02

between

HUSSEIN CHARGEER
of (or whose registered office is situated at)

1, LETSBY AVENUE, CRINGING, WILTS

(hereinafter called 'the Employer')

and

WESMEY-SHOVELGON LTD
of (or whose registered office is situated at)

2, THE BARRICADES, CRINGING, WILTS

(hereinafter called 'the Sub-Contractor')

(9/00)   Page

Whereas

First   the Sub-Contractor has submitted a tender on Tender NSC/T Part 2 (hereinafter called 'the Tender') on the terms and conditions in that Tender and in the Invitation to Tender NSC/T Part 1 to carry out works (as set out in the numbered tender documents enclosed therewith and referred to above and hereinafter called 'the Sub-Contract Works') as part of the Main Contract Works referred to above to be or being carried out on the terms and conditions relating thereto referred to in the Tender NSC/T Part 1 (hereinafter called 'the Main Contract'); and the Tender has been signed as 'approved' by or on behalf of the Employer;

Second   the Employer has appointed
FAIR AND SQUARE

to be the Architect/the Contract Administrator for the purposes of the Main Contract and this Agreement (hereinafter called 'the Architect/the Contract Administrator' which expression as used in this Agreement shall include his successors validly appointed under the Main Contract or otherwise if appointed before the Main Contract is operative);

Third   the Architect/the Contract Administrator on behalf of the Employer intends, after this Agreement has been executed and, if a Main Contract has not been entered into, after a Main Contract has been so entered into, to nominate the Sub-Contractor to carry out and complete the Sub-Contract Works on the terms and conditions of the Tender and the Invitation to tender NSC/T Part 1;

Fourth   nothing contained in this Agreement nor anything contained in the Tender or in the Invitation to Tender NSC/T Part 1 is intended to render the Architect/the Contract Administrator in any way liable to the Sub-Contractor in relation to matters in the said Agreement, Tender or Invitation to Tender;

Now it its hereby agreed

Completion of Sub-Contract: Sub-Contractor's obligations

1·1   The Sub-Contractor shall, after receipt of a copy of the Nomination Instruction (Nomination NSC/N) issued to the Main Contractor under clause 35·6 of the Main Contract Conditions, forthwith complete in agreement with the Main Contractor the Particular Conditions (NSC/T Part 3) and sign the completed NSC/T Part 3 or have it signed on his behalf and execute with the Main Contractor the Articles of Nominated Sub-Contract Agreement (Agreement NSC/A) unless, for good reasons stated in writing to the Main Contractor, the Sub-Contractor is unable to comply with this clause 1·1.

1·2   If the identity of the Main Contractor has not been notified in writing to the Sub-Contractor by the Employer or by the Architect/the Contract Administrator on his behalf before or on the date the Sub-Contractor signs this Agreement as a deed then, not later than 7 days after receipt by the Sub-Contractor of a written notification by the Employer or by the Architect/the Contract Administrator on his behalf of the identity of the person who becomes the Main Contractor, the Sub-Contractor may by notice in writing to the Employer state that:

·1   this Agreement shall cease to have effect except in respect of the warranty in clause 2·1 hereof and any amounts due under clause 2·2·2 hereof; and

·2   the OFFER on Tender NSC/T Part 2 is withdrawn notwithstanding any approval of that Tender by signature on page 8 thereof by or on behalf of the Employer.

1·3   If for any reason no Sub-Contract is entered into between a Main Contractor and the Sub-Contractor, this Agreement shall cease to have effect except in the respect of the warranty in clause 2·1 hereof and any amounts due under clause 2·2·2 hereof.

Design, selection of materials, satisfaction of performance specification – Sub-Contractor's warranty

2·1   The Sub-Contractor warrants that insofar as the Sub-Contract Works have been or will be designed by him he will comply with regulation 13 of the Construction (Design and Management) Regulations 1994 or any amendment or re-making thereof and, without prejudice to such compliance, warrants that he has exercised and will exercise all reasonable skill and care in

·1   the design of the Sub-Contract Works insofar as the Sub-Contract Works have been or will be designed by the Sub-Contractor; and

JCT

JCT Standard Form of Tender by Nominated Supplier

For use in connection with the Standard Form of Building Contract (SFBC) issued by the Joint Contracts Tribunal, 1980 edition, incorporating Amendments 1 to 9

Job Title: NEW DETACHED HOUSE
(name and brief location of Works)

1, LETSBY AVENUE, CRINGING, WILTS

[a] To be completed by or on behalf of the Architect/the Contract Administrator.

Employer: [a] HUSSEIN CHARGEER

1, LETSBY AVENUE, CRINGING, WILTS

Main Contractor: [a] WILLIAM DURR LTD
(if known)

2, THE BITTER END, CRINGING, WILTS

Tender for: [a] FITTED CARPET
(abbreviated description)

Name of Tenderer: WALTER WALL LTD

2, THE SKIRTING, CRINGING, WILTS

To be returned to: [a] FAIR AND SQUARE, 4, THE HELLOVET, CRINGING, WILTS

[b] To be completed by the supplier; see also Schedule 1, item 7.

Lump sum price: [b] £3,500.00

THREE THOUSAND AND FIVE HUNDRED POUNDS *(words)*
and/or Schedule of rates (attached)

---

[c] By SFBC clause 36·4·9 none of the provisions in the contract of sale can override, modify or affect in any way the provisions incorporated from SFBC clause 36·4 in that contract of sale. Nominated Suppliers should therefore take steps to ensure that their sale conditions do not incorporate any provisions which purport to override, modify or affect in any way the provisions incorporated from SFBC clause 36·4.

[d] May be completed by or on behalf of the Architect/the Contract Administrator; if not so completed, to be completed by the supplier.

[e] To be struck out by or on behalf of the Architect/the Contract Administrator if no Warranty Agreement is required.

1   We confirm that we will be under a contract with the Main Contractor:

·1   to supply the materials or goods described or referred to in **Schedule 1** for the price and/or at the rate set out above; and

·2   in accordance with the other terms set out in that Schedule, as a Nominated Supplier in accordance with the terms of SFBC clause 36·3 to ·5 (as set out in **Schedule 2**) and our conditions of sale in so far as they do not conflict with the terms of SFBC clause 36·3 to ·5[c]

provided:

·3   the Architect/the Contract Administrator has issued the relevant nomination instruction (a copy of which has been sent to us by the Architect/the Contract Administrator); and

·4   agreement on delivery between us and the Main Contractor has been reached as recorded in **Schedule 1** Part 6 (see SFBC clause 36·4·3); and

·5   we have thereafter received an order from the Main Contractor accepting this tender.

2   We agree that this Tender shall be open for acceptance by an order from the Main Contractor within _____ [d] of the date of this Tender. Provided that where the Main Contractor has not been named above we reserve the right to withdraw this Tender within 14 days of having been notified, by or on behalf of the Employer named above, of the name of the Main Contractor.

3[e]   Subject to our right to withdraw this Tender as set out in paragraph 2 we hereby declare that we accept the Warranty Agreement in the terms set out in **Schedule 3** hereto on condition that no provision in that Warranty Agreement shall take effect unless and until

a copy to us of the instruction nominating us,
the order of the Main Contract accepting this Tender, and
a copy of the Warranty Agreement signed by the Employer

have been received by us.

For and on behalf of   WALTER WALL LTD

Address   2, THE SKIRTINGS,
CRINGING, WILTS

Signature   W. Wall.   Date 6 August 2002

Schedule 3: Warranty Agreement by a Nominated Supplier

To the Employer: __HUSSEIN CHARGEER__

__1, LETSBY AVENUE, CRINGING, WILTS__

named in our Tender dated __6 AUGUST 2002__

For __FITTED CARPET TO LIVING AND DINING ROOMS AND__
(abbreviated description of goods/materials)

__THE HALL__

To be supplied to: __DETACHED HOUSE__
(job title)

__1, LETSBY AVENUE, CRINGING, WILTS__

1   Subject to the conditions stated in the above mentioned Tender (that no provision in this Warranty Agreement shall take effect unless and until the instruction nominating us, the order of the Main Contractor accepting the Tender and a copy of this Warranty Agreement signed by the Employer have been received by us) WE WARRANT in consideration of our being nominated in respect of the supply of the goods and/or materials to be supplied by us as a Nominated Supplier under the Standard Form of Building Contract referred to in the Tender and in accordance with the description, quantity and quality of the materials or goods and with the other terms and details set out in the Tender ('the supply') that:

1·1   We have exercised and will exercise all reasonable skill and care in:

1·1 ·1   the design of the supply insofar as the supply has been or will be designed by us; and

    ·2   the selection of materials and goods for the supply insofar as such supply has been or will be selected by us; and

    ·3   the satisfaction of any performance specification or requirement insofar as such performance specification or requirement is included or referred to in the Tender as part of the description of the supply.

1·2   We will:

1·2 ·1   save insofar as we are delayed by:

      ·1   force majeure; or

      ·2   civil commotion, local combination of workmen, strike or lock-out; or

      ·3   any instruction of the Architect/the Contract Administrator under SFBC clause 13·2 (Variations) or clause 13·3 (provisional sums); or

Pages 1 to 6 comprising Tender and Schedules 1 and 2 are issued in a separate pad, TNS/1 (SFBC).

1·2 ·1   continued

      ·4   failure of the Architect/the Contract Administrator to supply to us within due time any necessary information for which we have specifically applied in writing on a date which was neither unreasonably distant from nor unreasonably close to the date on which it was necessary for us to receive the same

    so supply the Architect/the Contract Administrator with such information as the Architect/the Contract Administrator may reasonably require; and

    ·2   so supply the Contractor with such information as the Contractor may reasonably require in accordance with the arrangements in our contract of sale with the Contractor; and

    ·3   so commence and complete delivery of the supply in accordance with the arrangements in our contract of sale with the Contractor

    that the Contractor shall not become entitled to an extension of time under SFBC clauses 25·4·6 or 25·4·7 of the Main Contract Conditions nor become entitled to be paid for direct loss and/or expense ascertained under SFBC clause 26·1 for the matters referred to in clause 26·2·1 of the Main Contract Conditions; and we will indemnify you to the extent but not further or otherwise that the Architect/the Contract Administrator is obliged to give an extension of time so that the Employer is unable to recover damages under the Main Contract for delays in completion, and/or pay an amount in respect of direct loss and/or expense as aforesaid because of any failure by us under clause 1·2·1 or 1·2·2 hereof.

2   We have noted the amount of the liquidated and ascertained damages under the Main Contract, as stated in TNS/1 Schedule 1, item 8.

3   Nothing in the Tender is intended to or shall exclude or limit our liability for breach of the warranties set out above.

4·1   In case any dispute or difference shall arise between the Employer or the Architect/the Contract Administrator on his behalf and ourselves as to any matter or thing of whatsoever nature arising out of this Agreement or in connection therewith then such dispute or difference shall be and is hereby referred to arbitration. When we or the Employer require such dispute or difference to be referred to arbitration we or the Employer shall given written notice to the other to such effect and such dispute or difference shall be referred to the arbitration and final decision of a person to be agreed between the parties as the Arbitrator, or, upon failure so to agree within 14 days after the date of the aforesaid written notice, of a person to be appointed as the Arbitrator on the request of either ourselves or the Employer by the person named in the Appendix to the Standard Form of Building Contract referred to in the Tender.

4·2 ·1   Provided that if the dispute or difference to be referred to arbitration under this Agreement raises issues which are substantially the same as or connected with the issues raised in a related dispute between the Employer and the Contractor under the Main Contract or between a Nominated Sub-Contractor and the Contractor under Sub-Contract NSC/4 or NSC/4a or between the Employer and any other Nominated Supplier, and if the related dispute has also been referred for determination to an Arbitrator, the Employer and ourselves hereby agree that the dispute or difference under this Agreement shall be referred to the Arbitrator appointed to determine the related dispute; and the JCT Arbitration Rules applicable to the related dispute shall apply to the dispute under this Agreement; and such Arbitrator shall have power to make such directions and all necessary awards in the same way as if the procedure of the High Court as to joining one or more of the defendants or joining co-defendants or third parties was available to the parties and to him; and the agreement of consent referred to in paragraph 4·6 on appeals or applications to the High Court on any question of law shall apply to any question of law arising out of the awards of such Arbitrator in respect of all related disputes referred to him or arising in the course of the reference of all the related disputes referred to him.

    ·2   Save that the Employer or ourselves may require the dispute or difference under this Agreement to be referred to a different Arbitrator (to be appointed under this Agreement) if either of us reasonably considers that the Arbitrator appointed to determine the related dispute is not properly qualified to determine the dispute or difference under this Agreement.

    ·3   Paragraphs 4·2·1 and 4·2·2 hereof shall apply unless in the Appendix to the Standard Form of Building Contract referred to in the Tender the words 'clause 41·2·1 and 41·2·2 apply' have been deleted.

4·3   Such reference shall not be opened until after Practical Completion or alleged Practical Completion of the Main Contract Works or termination or alleged termination of the Contractor's employment under the Main Contract or abandonment of the Main Contract Works, unless with the written consent of the Employer or the Architect/the Contract Administrator on his behalf and ourselves.

4·4   Subject to paragraph 4·5 the award of such Arbitrator shall be final and binding on the parties.

4·5   The parties hereby agree and consent pursuant to Sections 1(3) and 2(1) (b) of the Arbitration Act, 1979, that either party

    ·1   may appeal to the High Court on any question of law arising out of an award made in any arbitration under this Arbitration Agreement; and

    ·2   may apply to the High Court to determine any question of law arising in the course of the reference;

    and the parties agree that the High Court should have jurisdiction to determine any such question of law.

4·6   Whatever the nationality, residence or domicile of ourselves or the Employer, the Contractor, any sub-contractor or supplier or the Arbitrator, and wherever the Works or any part thereof are situated, the law of England shall be the proper law of this Warranty and in particular (but not so as to derogate from the generality of the foregoing) the provisions of the Arbitration Acts 1950 (notwithstanding anything in S.34 thereof) to 1979 shall apply to any arbitration under this Contract wherever the same, or any part of it, shall be conducted.[*]

4·7   If before his final award the Arbitrator dies or otherwise ceases to act as the Arbitrator, the Employer and ourselves shall forthwith appoint a further Arbitrator, or, upon failure so to appoint within 14 days of any such death or cessation, then either the Employer or ourselves may request the person named in the Appendix to the Standard Form of Building Contract referred to in the Tender to appoint such further Arbitrator. Provided that no such further Arbitrator shall be entitled to disregard any direction of the previous Arbitrator or to vary or revise any award of the previous Arbitrator except to the extent that the previous Arbitrator had power so to do under the JCT Arbitration Rules and/or with the agreement of the parties and/or by the operation of law.

4·8   The arbitration shall be conducted in accordance with the 'JCT Arbitration Rules' current at the date of the Tender. Provided that if any amendments to the Rules so current have been issued by the Joint Contracts Tribunal after the aforesaid date the Employer and Supplier may, by a joint notice in writing to the Arbitrator, state that they wish the arbitration to be conducted in accordance with the JCT Arbitration Rules as so amended.[†]

[††]Signature of or on behalf of the Supplier: _W. Wall_

[††]Signature of or on behalf of the Employer: _H Chargeer_

[*] Where the parties do not wish the proper law of the Warranty to be the law of England appropriate amendments to paragraph 4·7 should be made. Where the Works are situated in Scotland then the forms issued by the Scottish Building Contract Committee which contain Scots proper law and arbitration provisions are the appropriate documents. It should be noted that the provisions of the Arbitration Acts 1950 to 1979 do not apply to arbitrations conducted in Scotland.

[†] The JCT Arbitration Rules contain stricter time limits than those prescribed by some arbitration rules or those frequently observed in practice. The parties should note that a failure by a party or the agent of a party to comply with the time limits incorporated in these Rules may have adverse consequences.

[††] If the Warranty Agreement is to be executed as a deed advice should be sought on the correct method of execution.

TELEPHONE MESSAGE

Time 10.30.a.m.   Date 8.OCT.02

From Arthur Bitter   To Bill F.
(builder)

Concerning

Tenders for the Council job

He says he has discovered a substantial
error in his bid, which was accepted
yesterday. Can he change it?

Taken By V.N.

1, Forthey Road
Cringing
Wilts

October 16th

Dear Mr Square,

Regarding the project in the neighbouring
plot at 3, Forthey Road; I have been through the
Standard Form of Building Contract (Private with
Quantities) which you suggested we use, and find I
am not satisfied with several of the conditions.

I enclose a revised copy containing amendments
and additions which I have made. I think we should
use this instead.

Yours truly,

O. fforagh-Nuther

O. fforagh-Nuther

MEMO

To   : TOM SQUARE

From   : ROY TRINC

Date   : OCT.21.

Concerning : TYPE OF CONTRACT

WE'VE BEEN ASKED TO DEAL WITH THE RENOVATION OF
A DILAPIDATED COACH-HOUSE. THE OWNER WANTS TO
CONVERT IT INTO A RESTAURANT/PRIVATE CLUB, AND
WANTS TO OPEN AS SOON AS POSSIBLE - WHAT SORT OF
CONTRACT SHOULD WE ADVISE?

R.T.

DESK DIARY

OCT 21

re: Bitter's errors.
Contractually, the agreement is binding but in the Selective Tendering Code, errors are dealt with in this case under Alternative I, so that the employer could have allowed a change, but too late now. Anyway, not our problem; Inform the Council & wait for instructions before proceeding.

OCT 22

re: fforagh-Nuther's alterations to Standard Form.
Write & dissuade — Fiddling with the standard clauses is asking for trouble.

OCT 23

re: Coach-house renovation
Suggest Cost + Fluctuating fee contract.
The work will be tricky and it's unlikely that we can get an accurate price at the outset. The Fluctuating fee will a) help to keep the cost down.
b) Make sure the work's done as fast as possible.

Fair and Square

CHARTERED ARCHITECTS

B.FAIR.dip.arch.RIBA.
T.SQUARE.B.Arch.RIBA.AFAS.

BF/vn

4, The Hellovet,
Cringing,
Wilts.

23.10.02

Dear Mr fforagh-Nuther,

Re : Proposed House at 3 Forthey Road

Thank you for your letter of the 16th October. With regard to the amendments you propose, we would strongly advise that you consider the consequences of such an action. The Standard Form is a complex, comprehensive document containing many inter-dependent conditions. They have been drafted under expert guidance, based on detailed knowledge of the construction process, and any interference with the accepted format may lead to incalculable consequences later in the project.

The changes you propose do not seem to merit the problems they may cause, and we would not really be happy to proceed, at least until professional legal advice has been taken. May we suggest that, if you are convinced that the Standard Form is inadequate, it would be to our mutual benefit if you sought legal assistance in this matter.

We look forward to hearing from you,

Yours sincerely,

Fair & Square

Fair and Square

O. fforagh-Nuther
1 Forthey Road
Cringing
Wilts

THE CONSTRUCTION PHASE

Contents

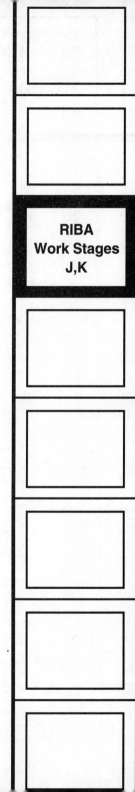

**RIBA
Work Stages
J,K**

Progress Appraisal

The progress of operations on site may be assessed and monitored by a number of mechanisms including:
- site reports
- the contractor's programme
- site visits
- meetings
- expenditure forecast compared with actual certification

Site reports

Site reports are written by the clerk of works (if employed) or the site supervisor, and submitted weekly to the architect, constituting a detailed record of the job. The site report might include:
- contractor's workforce per day;
- sub-contractor's workforce per day;
- plant and materials delivered to the site;
- plant removed from the site;
- shortages, stoppages and delays;
- weather report and temperature details;
- site visitors and meetings;
- dates of information required and drawings, Architect's Instructions etc. received;
- general progress and observation.

CLERK OF WORKS REPORT

The programme

The contractor's programme (see page 63), can be used as a means of assessing the contractor's performance in relation to original estimates and intentions, and in relation to the site reports. This is particularly easy if the programme is computerised.

Site visits

Site visits are dealt with on page 76.

Meetings

Meetings may be held periodically between various parties during the construction process. Types of meetings include:
- PROJECT MEETINGS, for architectural staff to discuss the particular project;
- CONTRACTOR MEETINGS, held between the contractor and sub-contractors (and the architect may attend if asked), preferably just prior to the
- MAIN SITE MEETINGS, which may be held:
  - at regular intervals
  - at specific times in the construction process
  - when problems occur
  - when it seems necessary to provide impetus.

Those attending, in addition to the architect and the contractor may include:
- the employer and/or project manager
- the user
- the clerk of works
- the quantity surveyor
- various consultants

Procedure

Whoever takes reponsibility for chairing a site meeting (usually the architect) will prepare and distribute the minutes not more than 7 days after the event. Dissents should be registered immediately.

All parties due to attend should be notified 7 days prior to the proposed meeting unless the date has already been fixed at the previous meeting.

The agenda

At the meeting:
- take the names of those present;
- give the names of those sending apologies.

AGENDA:
- Agree minutes of the last meeting, or deal with any problems arising from them.
- Contractor's report.
- Clerk of works' report (if employed).
- Consultants' reports.
- Quantity surveyor's report.
- Communication and procedures: any action required, by whom, etc.
- Contract progress.
- Any other business.
- Time and place of next meeting.

AGENDA

JOB TITLE : _____   JOB CODE : ___

PROGRESS MEETING No : _____

1. Agreement to minutes of Meeting No . . . held on . . .
2. Matters arising.
3. Progress to date.
   3.1 Contractors
   3.2 Clerk of Works
   3.3 Consultants
   3.4 Q.S.
4. Matters affecting progress.
5. Any other business.
6. Date of next meeting.

DISTRIBUTION :

Employer	I	Elec. Con.	I
Contractor	I	Structural Con.	I
Q S	I	Clerk of Works	I
Mech. Con.	I	File	I

References

ARCHITECT IN PRACTICE, pp. 248–57.
ARCHITECT'S GUIDE TO RUNNING A JOB, pp. 112–9.

Contract variations

Despite the preparation of detailed drawings and bills, it is possible that the quality or quantity of the proposed work agreed upon in the contract documents will need to be changed. Contractually, the contractor need do nothing that is not agreed upon, and so the contract (Standard Form) contains a provision allowing for additions, alterations and omissions from the originally proposed work.

The need for a variation may stem from:
- inadequate design work;
- changes of mind or opinion after the contract has been signed;
- unforeseen circumstances.

Definition

A variation provision has only limited scope and cannot, for example, be used to change the essence of the contract. If such a fundamental change was required, it would be necessary to determine the contract by mutual consent, and draft a new one.

A variation is an 'alteration or modification of the design, quality or quantity of the Works as shown upon the Contract Drawings and described by or referred to in the Contract Bills' (Standard Form clause 13.1.1.), or the imposition, variation or omission of restrictions (Standard Form clause 13.1.2.).

Dependent upon the characteristics of the change required, it may be difficult to determine whether a variation is necessary. For example, if the job cost more than the contractor expected, this would not be grounds for a variation (although it may be dealt with under a fluctuations clause).

Authorisation

If the work qualifies for a variation, a written order is required to justify payment. For this purpose, it is advisable to use an Architect's Instruction (see page 75). The architect's signature must always appear by way of authorisation. If the clerk of works issues a direction it is of no effect unless confirmed by the architect in writing within 2 days.

Cost

The cost of a variation may be calculated by:
- an agreed price;
- measurement and valuation by a third party, e.g. a quantity surveyor;
- reference to the Contract Bill rates, varied if necessary to suit changes in conditions;
- using a fair and reasonable price basis;
- daywork rates plus a percentage addition in accordance with the contract.

Within the standard form, there are a number of mechanisms for valuing variations or possible variations. These are set out in clause 13. Clause 13.4 sets out two alternatives: A and B. Alternative A provides that within 21 days of an instruction or upon the further receipt of sufficient information, the contractor can submit a price statement. This statement sets out not only the price for the variation to the work but also any extension of time and loss and/or expense sought. Within a further 21 days, the quantity surveyor after consultation with the architect is to inform the contractor that the price statement is accepted, accepted in part or not accepted. The quantity surveyor in this notification should set out reasons as to why the statement has been rejected either in whole or in part, and supply an alternative statement. The contractor has 14 days in which to accept or reject the amended statement. Should either party not accept the statement or the amended version, the matter is referable to adjudication. If the contractor attaches quotations for extensions of time and loss and/or expense to the statement, then again within the 21 day period the quantity surveyor notifies the contractor whether the quotation or quotations are accepted. If the quantity surveyor does not respond within the 21 day period, the statement is treated as if the quotation or quotations were not attached. A failure to agree the statement or amended statement results in alternative B applying. Alternative B is the commonly adopted approach of the quantity surveyor, valuing the additional work on the basis of bill rates, suitably amended bills rates given the nature of the works, reasonable rates or daywork rates.

Under clause 13A it is possible to invite quotations (13A quotations) from the contractor before the work is instructed, unlike alternative A where the instruction is issued. A 13A quotation should set out the basis of the valuation (e.g. bill rates, supporting information, including the valuation of preliminaries, any extension of time sought and loss and/or expense sought), and a fair and reasonable cost to prepare the valuation. If within 7 days of the receipt of the quotation by the quantity surveyor the employer does not accept the contractor's quotation, the architect should either issue an instruction stating that the variation is not to be carried out or that it is to be carried out and valued under clause 13.4.

Effects

Authorisation of a variation may result in:
- increased cost to the client;
- increased time necessary to complete which may affect:
  - insurances
  - bonuses
  - hire charges
  - extra fees (architect, clerk of works)
  - other expenditures or financial loss (e.g. loss of potential rent, moving expenses, etc.)

in which case the employer must be informed, and the quantity surveyor notified to assess the situation and its consequences.

Provisions

Variations are often instructed against:
- provisional sums in the contract. These are sums provided for work or for costs which cannot be entirely foreseen, e.g. for work of an experimental nature.
- prime cost sums, i.e. sums of money included in the contract to be expended on materials from suppliers or work carried out by nominated sub-contractors.

It is possible for a provisional sum to become a prime cost sum upon the issuance of an Architect's Instruction to that effect.

(Continued from page 73)

The Architect's Instruction

The RIBA produce a standard Architect's Instruction form which may conveniently be used for a number of matters including:

- errors in Bills of Quantities (c.2.2.2.2);
- discrepancies between the contract drawings and the Bills of Quantities (c.2.3);
- statutory obligations (c.6.1.3);
- errors in setting out not to be amended and adjustment to Contract Sum (c.7);
- opening up, inspection and testing (c.8.3);
- removal of materials and goods not in accordance with the contract (c.8.4);
- variations after discovery of defective work (c.8.4.3);
- opening up, inspection and testing after discovery of defective work (c.8.4.4);
- variations if work not carried out in a proper and workmanlike manner (c.8.5);
- exclusion of persons from the works (c.8.6);
- confirmation of a clerk of works; direction (c.12);
- requirement or sanction of variations (c.13.2);
- expenditure of provisional sums included in the Contract Bills (c.13.3.1);
- expenditure or provisional sums included in a sub-contract (c.13.3.2);
- sanctioning the removal of unfixed materials and goods from site (c.16.1);
- schedule of defects (c.17.2);
- requirement that defects be made good within the Defects Liability Period or that they are not to be made good, and an appropriate adjustment be made to the Contract Sum (c.17.3);
- postponement of work (c.23.2);
- discovery of antiquities (c.34.2);
- removing objection to sub-contractor (c.35.5.2);
- omitting work of sub-contractor or to requiring selection of another sub-contractor (c.35.9.2);
- requiring contractor to give sub-contractor notice specifying the relevant default (c.35.24.6.1);
- nominating suppliers (c.36.2)

References

THE ARCHITECT IN PRACTICE, pp. 260–4.

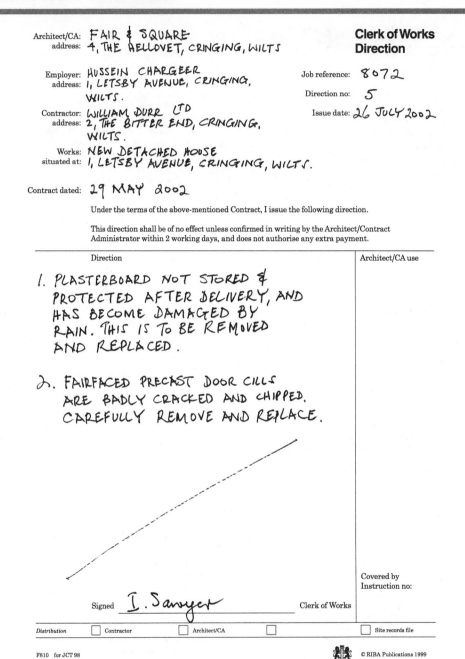

Architect/CA: FAIR & SQUARE
address: 4, THE HELLOVET, CRINGING, WILTS

Clerk of Works Direction

Employer: HUSSEIN CHARGEER
address: 1, LETSBY AVENUE, CRINGING, WILTS.

Job reference: 8072

Contractor: WILLIAM DURR LTD
address: 2, THE BITTER END, CRINGING, WILTS.

Direction no: 5

Issue date: 26 JULY 2002

Works: NEW DETACHED HOUSE
situated at: 1, LETSBY AVENUE, CRINGING, WILTS.

Contract dated: 29 MAY 2002

Under the terms of the above-mentioned Contract, I issue the following direction.

This direction shall be of no effect unless confirmed in writing by the Architect/Contract Administrator within 2 working days, and does not authorise any extra payment.

Direction	Architect/CA use
1. PLASTERBOARD NOT STORED & PROTECTED AFTER DELIVERY, AND HAS BECOME DAMAGED BY RAIN. THIS IS TO BE REMOVED AND REPLACED. 2. FAIRFACED PRECAST DOOR CILLS ARE BADLY CRACKED AND CHIPPED. CAREFULLY REMOVE AND REPLACE.	Covered by Instruction no:

Signed I. Sawyer Clerk of Works

| Distribution | ☐ Contractor | ☐ Architect/CA | ☐ | ☐ Site records file |

F810 for JCT 98   © RIBA Publications 1999

Issued by: FAIR AND SQUARE
address: 4, THE HELLOVET, CRINGING, WILTS

**Architect's
Instruction**

Employer: HUSSEIN CHARGEER
address: 1, LETSBY AVENUE, CRINGING, WILTS

Job reference: 8072

Instruction no: 18

Contractor: WILLIAM DURR LTD
address: 2, THE BITTER END, CRINGING, WILTS

Issue date: 27 JULY 2002

Sheet: 1   of 1

Works: NEW DETACHED HOUSE
situated at: 1, LETSBY AVENUE, CRINGING, WILTS

Contract dated: 29 MAY 2002

Under the terms of the above-mentioned Contract, I/we issue the following instructions:

	Office use: Approximate costs	
	£ omit	£ add
1. We confirm the issue of the Clerk of Works Direction No. 5 dated 26 July 2002.		
2. We confirm our oral instruction to you on 25 July 2002, to take down and remove from site the screen wall, which was not built in accordance with the drawings and specification, and rebuild. This work is to be carried out at your own expense.		

To be signed by or for the issuer named above

Signed *Fair & Square*

Amount of Contract Sum	£	
± Approximate value of previous Instructions	£	
Sub-total	£	
± Approximate value of this Instruction	£	
Approximate adjusted total	£	

Distribution

☐ Contractor ☐ Quantity Surveyor ☐ Clerk of Works ☐

☐ Employer ☐ Structural Engineer ☐ Planning Supervisor ☐

☐ Nominated Sub-Contractors ☐ M&E Consultant ☐ ☐ File

F809 for JCT 98 / IFC 98 / MW 98

© RIBA Publications 1999

The Architect's Duties

Although not a party to the building contract, the architect, in the role of agent, has several duties to perform in the construction process. The designated powers which create these duties are stated in the Conditions of the Standard Form (over 50 exist), and care should be taken not to exceed jurisdiction by doing anything which, although seemingly relevant, forms no part of the architect's actual duties. For example, if asked for advice on how to build a part of the project, the architect should decline, remembering that it is the contractor's contractual obligation to ensure compliance with contract documents.

The architect's duties cover two principal areas:
PERFORMANCE EVALUATION
CERTIFICATION

Performance evaluation

In evaluating the contractor's performance, the architect plays two distinct roles:
- INSPECTOR: Where so required by the contract, the architect must check that certain work is in absolute accordance with the contract documents.
- JUDGE: Other clauses of the Standard Form require the architect to provide a qualitative opinion on work. The clauses imposing this duty are phrased 'to the architect's satisfaction'.

In order that these duties may be fulfilled, certain powers are granted to the architect by the Standard Form including:
- the ordering of tests to be made on goods, materials or workmanship;
- the requiring of proof of compliance of goods or materials with the contract documents;
- the ordering of work to be uncovered for inspection;
- the ordering of work that is not in accordance with the contract to be removed;
- the ordering of any person on site who is not working to the architect's satisfaction to be removed.

Certification

(see page 57).

At prescribed stages in the construction programme, the architect is empowered to check the work completed to date. If it is determined to be in accordance with the contract, the value of the work is calculated (frequently by the quantity surveyor). The architect must then issue an Interim Certificate (see page 77), to be sent to the employer, with copies for the quantity surveyor, the contractor and the file. The employer is obliged to pay the certified amount within 14 days. At the same time, the architect sends a Notification to the nominated sub-contractors indicating the issuance of the certificate, and directions to the contractor to pay the sub-contractors the relevant amount.

Prior to 1974, the architect had a quasi-arbitral immunity in respect of claims arising out of negligent certification (see page 6). Since the removal of this protection, great care should be exercised before issuing any certificate and the quantity surveyor should be given a list of defective work each month with instructions to omit such work from the valuation.

Site visits

Periodical site visits should be made by the architect, and the intervals will depend upon a number of factors including:
- type and complexity of the project;
- nature of the employer;
- personal knowledge of the contractor;
- locality of the site;
- whether or not a clerk of works is employed;
- particular events, for example, the arrival of equipment;
- unforeseen events, for example, bad weather;
- the stage of the work reached.

On arrival, the architect should inform the person in charge of their presence, and remember only to deal with them (or their representative) during the visit. An inspection plan should be prepared before work commences on site and a record should be kept of all site visits, noting any observations, information supplied, and actions to be taken. A copy of the record may then be sent to the quantity surveyor.

```
                SITE  VISIT  REPORT
Job Title . . . . . . . .      Job No. . . . . . .
Site Visit No . . . . .          Date . . . . . . .
Name . . . . . . . . . . . Distribution . . . . . . .

Purpose of  Visit :


Observations :



Action  Required / Taken :
```

Visits might arise out of the following:
- Positioning of site huts.
- Establishment of datum points, bench marks and building layout.
- Dimensions and grades.
- Safety and security provisions.
- Protection of trees etc.
- Fences, hoardings, signs etc.
- Siting of spoil heaps.
- Excavations and soil underfootings.
- Testing of drainage.
- Public utility connections.
- Foundations, reinforcement, pile driving, caissons.
- Concrete tests, formwork, reinforcement.
- Structural frames.
- Floor openings, sleeves and hangers.
- Quality and placing of concrete.
- Weather precautions.
- Masonry layout, materials.
- Bonding and flashing.
- Frames and prefabricated elements.
- Partition layout.
- Temporary enclosures, heat and light.
- Protection of finished work.
- Partitions and plasterwork.
- Titles, electrical work and wiring.

References

THE ARCHITECT IN PRACTICE, pp. 248–50, 255–6.
ARCHITECT'S HANDBOOK OF PRACTICE MANAGEMENT, pp. 295–8.
THE ARCHITECT'S GUIDE TO RUNNING A JOB, pp. 128–35.

**Interim
Certificate**

and Direction

`JCT 98`

Issued by: FAIR AND SQUARE
address: 4, THE HELLOVET, CRINGING, WILTS

Employer: HUSSEIN CHARGEER
address: 1, LETSBY AVENUE, CRINGING, WILTS

Serial no: **G 111438**

Job reference: 8072

Contractor: WILLIAM DURR LTD
address: 2, THE BITTER END, CRINGING, WILTS

Certificate no: 8

Date of valuation: 1 October 2002

Works: NEW DETACHED HOUSE
situated at: 1, LETSBY AVENUE, CRINGING, WILTS

Date of issue: 8 October 2002

Final date for payment: 22 October 2002

Contract dated: 29 May 2002

Original to Employer

This Interim Certificate is issued under the terms of the above-mentioned Contract.

Gross valuation	£198,000.00
Less Retention as detailed on the Statement of Retention	£ 9,900.00
Sub-total	£188,100.00
Less reimbursement of advance payment	£ -----
Sub-total	£188,100.00
Less total amount previously certified	£160,000.00
Net amount for payment	£ 28,100.00

I/We hereby certify that the **amount due** to the Contractor from the Employer is (in words)

All amounts are exclusive of VAT.

TWENTY EIGHT THOUSAND ONE HUNDRED POUNDS ONLY

I/We hereby direct the Contractor that this amount includes interim or final payments to Nominated Sub-Contractors as listed in the attached *Statement of Retention and of Nominated Sub-Contractor's Values*, which are to be paid to those named in accordance with the Sub-Contract.

To be signed by or for the issuer named above

Signed *Fair & Square*

[1] Relevant only if clause 1A of the VAT Agreement applies. Delete if not applicable.

[1] The Contractor has given notice that the rate of VAT chargeable on the supply of goods and services to which the Contract relates is _____ %

[1] _____ % of the amount certified above .... £ _____

[1] Total of net amount and VAT amount (for information) .... £ _____

This is not a Tax Invoice.

F801 for JCT 98

© RIBA Publications 1999

Issued by: FAIR AND SQUARE
address: 4, THE HELLOVET, CRINGING, WILTS

Notification
to Nominated
Sub-Contractor
of amount included
in certificate

Employer: HUSSEIN CHARGEER
address: 1, LETSBY AVENUE, CRINGING, WILTS

Job reference: 8072

Notification no: 2

Main Contractor: WILLIAM DURR LTD
address: 2, THE BITTER END, CRINGING, WILTS

Issue date: 8 October 2002

Works: NEW DETACHED HOUSE
situated at: 1, LETSBY AVENUE, CRINGING, WILTS

Contract dated: 29 May 2002

Original to Nominated
Sub-Contractor

Nominated
Sub-Contractor: WESMEY-SHOVELGON LTD
address: 2, THE BARRICADES, CRINGING, WILTS

Under the terms of the above-mentioned Main Contract,

I/we hereby inform you that I/we have directed the Contractor that

Interim Certificate no. 8 dated 8 October 2002

*Delete as
appropriate

includes *an interim/fixed payment of .... £ 2,350.00
which is to be discharged to you.

To be signed by or for
the issuer named
above

Signed _Fair & Square_

- -

Main Contractor: WILLIAM DURR LTD
address: 2, THE BITTER END, CRINGING, WILTS

Nominated Sub-Contractor's
**Acknowledgement
of Discharge**
of payment due

Works: NEW DETACHED HOUSE
situated at: 1, LETSBY AVENUE, CRINGING, WILTS

Job reference: 8072

In accordance with the terms of the relevant Sub-Contract,
we confirm that we have received from you discharge of the amount of ..... £ 2,350.00

included in Interim Certificate no. 8 dated 8 October 2002

as stated in Notification no. 2 dated 8 October 2002

Please complete
acknowledgement slip
and send to
Contractor

Signed _W. Wen_ Date 22·10·02

For Wesmey-Shovelgon Ltd

F803 for JCT 80

© RIBA Publications Ltd 1993

Issued by: FAIR AND SQUARE
address: 4, THE HELLOVET, CRINGING, WILTS

Works: NEW DETACHED HOUSE
situated at: 1, LETSBY AVENUE, CRINGING, WILTS

Statement of Retention
and of Nominated Sub-Contractors' Values

Job reference: 8072
Relating to Certificate no: 8
Issue date: 8 October 2002

| | Gross valuation | Amount subject to: | | | Amount of retention | Net valuation | Previously certified | Balance due |
		Full retention of 5 %	Half retention of %	Nil retention				
	£	£	£	£	£	£	£	£
Main Contractor								
WILLIAM DURR LTD	195,000	195,000	–	–	9,750	185,250	159,500	25,750
Nominated Sub-Contractors:								
WESMEY-SHOVELGON LTD	3,000	3,000	–	–	150	2,850	500	2,350
Total	198,000	198,000	–	–	9,900	188,100	160,000	28,100

All amounts are exclusive of VAT

F802   for JCT 80

No account has been taken of any discounts for cash to which the Contractor may be entitled if discharging the balance within 17 days of the issue of the Interim Certificate.

Delays

Dealing with delays

Building contracts generally stipulate a completion date in the Appendix. If the contractor does not finish within the time allocated, the Contract has been breached. Several mechanisms exist in the 1998 Standard Form of Building Contract (JCT – Private with Quantities) to deal with delays:

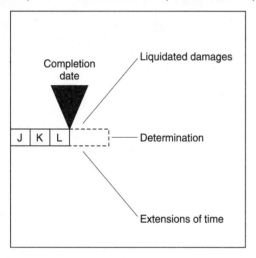

Liquidated damages (Clause 24)

These are specified in the Appendix, and provide for an agreed sum to be paid by the contractor for every day or week that completion is overdue.

Determination

In certain circumstances, the contractor's employment under the contract may be determined (see page 94).

Extensions of time (Clause 25)

Should the date for completion be delayed by virtue of an agreed clause, the contract time may be extended accordingly. Examples of events which might entail an extension of time include:
- force majeure;
- deferment of possession;

- exceptionally adverse weather conditions;
- loss or damage by specified perils;
- civil commotion, strikes etc.;
- compliance with certain Architect's Instructions:
  - discrepancies 2.3, 2.4.1
  - variations 13.2, 13A.4.1
  - provisional sums 13.3
  - postponement 23.2
  - antiquities 34
  - nominated sub-contractors 35
  - nominated suppliers 36
  - opening up 8.3
- information not received in time;
- delay by a nominated sub-contractor or nominated supplier (provided that the contractor has made every practicable effort to reduce such delay);
- work or materials which the employer has supplied or failed to supply;
- exercise of statutory powers by government;
- effects of statutory obligations;
- unforeseen labour shortages or material shortages;
- employer's failure to give necessary access to and from the site;
- approximate quantities not reasonably accurately forecast;
- change to performance specified work resulting from changes to statutory requirements;
- use or threat of terrorism;
- compliance with CDM Regulations;
- suspension by contractor of their obligations.

It is the duty of the contractor to use 'best endeavors' to prevent any delay, but if the delay is inevitable then, in order to be entitled to an extension of time, the contractor must:
- give a written notice to the architect whenever a delay occurs or is expected, stating the cause and specifying the Relevant Event (as listed above) if appropriate;
- where a nominated sub-contractor is involved, give a copy of the notice to them;
- the expected effects of any Relevant Event must be detailed (either in the notice or as soon as possible afterwards) with an estimated delay time;
- notify any change in circumstances or estimates.

Note that every delay must be notified, even those which are clearly the fault of the contractor.

The architect will then assess the notification, requiring such proof as deemed necessary (e.g. claims due to adverse weather may need to be supported by meteorological reports), and make a 'fair and reasonable' decision. The architect should

notify the contractor of the new completion date stating which relevant events have been taken into account. The new date must be fixed not later than 12 weeks from receipt of the details or, on a project with less than 12 weeks left to the original completion date, not later than that original date. Nominated sub-contractors should also be notified in writing of any architect's decision with regard to the completion date, and the contractor must be notified if no extension is to be granted. At any time after the Contract Completion Date, but not later than 12 weeks *after* Practical Completion, the architect must review the situation and issue a notice:
- fixing a new date for completion even if no notification has been received;
- confirming the existing date;
- fixing an earlier date, having regard to recent instructions.

Specified perils

- Fire
- Lightning
- Explosion
- Storm
- Tempest
- Flood
- Bursting or overflowing of water tanks, apparatus or pipes
- Earthquake
- Aircraft and other aerial devices or articles dropped therefrom
- Riot and civil commotion

Excluding any loss or damage caused by:
- Ionising radiations
- Contamination by radioactivity from any nuclear fuel or from any nuclear waste from the combustion of nuclear fuel, radioactive toxic explosive or other hazardous properties of any explosive nuclear assembly or nuclear component thereof
- Pressure waves caused by aircraft or other aerial devices travelling at sonic or supersonic speeds.

References

THE ARCHITECT IN PRACTICE, pp. 277–9.
THE ARCHITECT'S GUIDE TO RUNNING A JOB, pp. 78–9.

Issued by: FAIR AND SQUARE
address: 4, THE HELLOVET, CRINGING, WILTS

Employer: HUSSEIN CHARGEER
address: 1, LETSBY AVENUE, CRINGING, WILTS

Contractor: WILLIAM DURR LTD
address: 2, THE BITTER END, CRINGING, WILTS

Works: NEW DETACHED HOUSE
situated at: 1, LETSBY AVENUE, CRINGING, WILTS

Contract dated: 29 May 2002

Notification of
Revision to

**Completion
Date**

JCT 98

Job reference: 8072

Notification no: 1.

Issue date: 15 July 2002

Under the terms of the above-mentioned Contract,

I/we give notice that the Completion Date for

*Delete as
appropriate

* the Works
* Section~~xxxxxxxxxxxxxxxxxxxxxxxxxxx of the Works~~

previously fixed as

17 December   20**02**

* is hereby fixed later than that previously fixed,
* ~~is hereby fixed earlier than that previously fixed~~
* ~~is hereby confirmed,~~

and is now

24 December   2002

* This revision has taken into account the following Relevant Events:

25.4.2 and 25.4.8.1.

* ~~This revision has taken into account the omission of work required by the following Instructions~~

* ~~This revision is made by reason of my/our review.~~

To be signed by or for
the issuer named
above

Signed *Fair & Square*

Distribution			
☑ Contractor	☑ Quantity Surveyor	☑ Clerk of Works	☐
☑ Employer	☐ Structural Engineer	☑ Planning Supervisor	☐
☑ Nominated Sub-Contractors	☐ M&E Consultant	☐	☑ File

F808   for JCT 98   © RIBA Publications 1999

Fair and Square

CHARTERED ARCHITECTS

B.FAIR.dip.arch.RIBA.
T.SQUARE.B.Arch.RIBA.AFAS.

4, The Hellovet,
Cringing,
Wilts.

BF/vn   12.8.02

Dear Mr Durr,
        re: Development at Letsby Avenue, Cringing

On behalf of the owner of the above property, Mr Hussein Chargeer,
I am confirming that he took possession of the garage and
detached workshop in accordance with Clause 18 of the Standard
Form of Contract on August 9th 2002.

        Yours sincerely,

        Fair & Square

        Fair and Square

William Durr Esq,
2, The Bitter End,
Cringing,
Wilts.

On some projects, it is possible that a part or portion of the works may be capable of occupancy by the owner prior to completion of the whole project. In this case, a 'written statement' is sent by the architect to the contractor confirming the date of possession and identifying the part of the work in question. It is also advisable for the architect to remind the owner of the transfer of insurance responsibilities for the occupied portion.

TELEPHONE MESSAGE

Date NOV.14.

e 3.30.p.m.

To BF/TS

om H.CHARGEER

Concerning

MR CHARGEER VISITED THE SITE YESTERDAY, AND WANTS A) A BAY WINDOW ADDED TO THE BEDROOM AND B) AN EXTRA WING ON THE BACK TO HOUSE A BILLIARD ROOM ETC.

WILL YOU DEAL WITH THIS FOR HIM?

Taken By V.N.

WESMEY-SHOVELGON LTD

Dear Messrs. Fair and Square,
I am writing to you in connection with the job in Letsby Avenue, where we are working as Nominated Sub-Contractors.

I acknowledge receipt of your Notification of issuance of the Certificate dated Oct. 8th. Unfortunately, we have not been paid yet, and all attempts on our part to contact Bill Durr have been snubbed. Could you help out on this one please?

Yours

J. Wesmey (Director)

P.S. I believe the carpeting supplier, Walter Wall is having similar problems.

P.P.S. I hear that Mr Square is converting a windmill for his own use. I'm sending over a few hundred quarries which should come in handy.

Reg. Office : 2, The Barricades, Cringing, Wilts.

WILLIAM DURR ESQ
Building Contractor

2, The Bitter End,
Cringing,
Wilts.

Dear Mr Fair,

re: Development at Letsby Avenue

25.11.02

In accordance with the Contract provisions, we are requesting a three week extension to the contract time to allow for a period of inclement weather, incorrect instructions from your good selves and a labour problems caused by manpower shortages and a wildcat strike.

Would you please alter the completion date accordingly?

Yours sincerely,

W.Durr.
W.Durr, LCIOB.

DESK DIARY

NOV 25

re: Wesmey-Shovelgon
NSC/W is in operation here, so we can
demand proof of payment from Durr- No proof,
and employer pays direct (35.13.5) Might also
mention supplier, but nothing we can do here.
Acknowledge Wesmey's letter, and tell him
what we are doing.

NOV 26

NO

Fair and Square

CHARTERED ARCHITECTS

4, The Hellovet,
Cringing,
Wilts.

B.FAIR.dip.arch.RIBA.
T.SQUARE.B.Arch.RIBA.AFAS.

26.11.02

BF/vn

Dear Mr Durr,   re: Development at Letsby Avenue, Cringing

We acknowledge receipt of your letter dated 25th November, the
contents of which we note. We would draw your attention to
Clause 25.2.1.1. of the Standard Form, and therefore require
further information concerning the material circumstances of
the delays you mention, and identification where appropriate
of the Relevant Event.

We also look forward to receiving as soon as possible
particulars of the anticipated effects of each Relevant Event
and your estimate of the expected delay in the completion of
the work.

We are confident that you will use your best efforts to
minimise the effects of any delays, and assure you of our prom
action as soon as we have heard from you.

Yours sincerely,

Fair & Square

Fair and Square

William Durr Esq,
2, The Bitter End,
Cringing,
Wilts.

Fair and Square

CHARTERED ARCHITECTS

B.FAIR.dip.arch.RIBA.
T.SQUARE.B.Arch.RIBA.AFAS.

4, The Hellovet,
Cringing,
Wilts.

BF/vn

15.11.02

Dear Mr Chargeer,
I received your telephone message
yesterday regarding a new bay window and an extra wing
to your new development in Letsby Avenue. Before
proceeding, we will have to check:
A) If the extra work will require
further Local Authority permissions.
B) Whether or not the additions you want
(particularly the new wing) constitute a 'material'
change to the contract, in which case a Variation will be
insufficient, and a new contract will have to be drawn up.
When we have established these points, we will be able
to advise you as to the added cost of the work, and the
extra time beyond the present Completion Date that wil
be necessary for design and construction

MEMO

To
From   : Tom
ate   : Bill
            : 20th Nov.
ncerning   : Wesmey's free Quarries
Have these arrived yet? A nice
thought, but you'd better send
them back (remember the
with profuse tha

SECTION SEVEN

COMPLETION

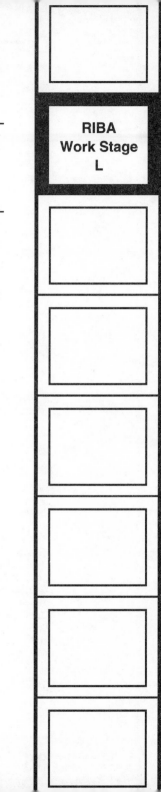

RIBA
Work Stage
L

Contents

Completion

Practical Completion (Clause 17)

When the work is completed except for very minor matters and there are no defects, the architect will inspect the work. If, in his or her opinion, all tests and inspections prove to be satisfactory, a Certificate of Practical Completion is issued. This has the effect of:

- allowing the release of half the retention sum, which the employer must pay within 14 days of the receipt by the employer of the next interim certificate (provisions may be made in the contract for the release of retained sums owing to sub-contractors who finish early);
- ending the responsibility of the employer or contractor to insure the property under the contract;
- enabling the employer to take possession, upon which the employer should adjust insurance cover accordingly;
- starting the Defects Liability Period which, if not specified in the Appendix, will be 6 months from the date of the Certificate of Practical Completion;
- ending the contractor's liability for liquidated damages;
- ending the contractor's liability for damage caused by frost occurring thereafter;
- ending the issue of regular interim certificates.

Defects Liability Period

Within 14 days of the expiration of this period, the architect must provide the contractor with a Schedule of Defects specifying any materials or workmanship not in accordance with the contract, including frost damage occurring prior to Practical Completion. The contractor must make good the defects within a reasonable time. At any time during the Defects Liability Period, the architect may require the making good of defects if considered necessary. When the work has been corrected to make it accord with the contract provisions, the architect will issue a Certificate of Making Good Defects. Upon issuance of this (or the expiration of the Defects Liability Period, whichever is the later), the architect authorises release of the balance of the retained sum in the next interim certificate.

With the employer's consent, the architect may instruct the contractor not to make good and an appropriate deduction is then made from the contract sum.

Final Certificate (Clause 30)

This is issued before the end of 2 months from the latest of the following:

- The end of the Defects Liability Period
- Issuance of the Making Good of Defects Certificate
- The sending of ascertainment and statement of final sum to the contractor.

A continuing liability period begins for the architect and the contractor as established by the Limitation Acts 1939 and 1980. This is normally 6 years, but extends to 12 years from Practical Completion if the contract is made as a deed. In tort, the position is more complex (see page 10).

Partial Possession (Clause 18)

The employer, with the contractor's consent (not to be unreasonably withheld) may take over a completed part of the building while the rest of the building work continues. The architect must issue a written statement identifying the part and the relevant date. Procedures are similar to Practical Completion, except that the value of the relevant part only is used for calculations, the amounts of retention and liquidated damages are proportionately reduced, and the contractor or the employer, as appropriate, reduces the amount of insurance accordingly.

Handover meetings

It may be convenient to hold a handover meeting at the end of the project, when inspections may be made and the building, site, owner's manual, keys, as-built drawings etc. passed into the employer's possession.

Extra services

Services offered by the architect after completion of the project might include:

- an evaluation of the structure in occupation;
- a maintenance contract of ongoing inspection at regular intervals.

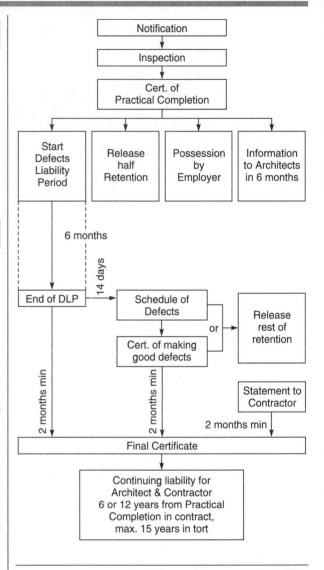

References

THE ARCHITECT'S GUIDE TO RUNNING A JOB, pp. 140–51.
THE ARCHITECT IN PRACTICE, pp. 287–302.

Issued by: FAIR AND SQUARE
address: 4, THE HELLOVET, CRINGING, WILTS

Employer: HUSSEIN CHARGEER
address: 1, LETSBY AVENUE, CRINGING, WILTS

Contractor: WILLIAM DURR LTD
address: 2, THE BITTER END, CRINGING, WILTS

Works: NEW DETACHED HOUSE
situated at: 1, LETSBY AVENUE, CRINGING, WILTS

Contract dated: 29 May 2002

Certificate of
**Practical
Completion**

JCT 98 / IFC 98

Job reference: 8072

Certificate no: 1.

Issue date: 24 January 2003

Under the terms of the above-mentioned Contract,

I/we hereby certify that in my/our opinion

Practical Completion of

* the Works

*Delete as appropriate

* Section xx xxxxxxxxxxxxxx of the Works

has been achieved

* and the Contractor has complied with the contractual requirements in respect of information for the health and safety file

This item applies to JCT 98 only.

* and the Contractor has supplied the specified drawings and information relating to Performance Specified Work

on 22 January   20 03

To be signed by or for the issuer named above

Signed *Fair & Square*

Distribution			
☑ Employer	☐ Structural Engineer	☑ Planning Supervisor	☐
☑ Contractor	☐ M&E Consultant	☐	☐
☑ Quantity Surveyor	☑ Clerk of Works	☐	☑ File

F853A/B for JCT 98 / IFC 98

© RIBA Publications 1999

Certificate of
Completion of

Making Good Defects

Issued by: FAIR AND SQUARE
address: 4, THE HELLOVET, CRINGING, WILTS

JCT 98

Employer: HUSSEIN CHARGEER
address: 1, LETSBY AVENUE, CRINGING, WILTS

Job reference: 8072

Contractor: WILLIAM DURR LTD
address: 2, THE BITTER END, CRINGING, WILTS

Certificate no: 1 .

Issue date: 26 August 2003

Works: NEW DETACHED HOUSE
situated at: 1, LETSBY AVENUE, CRINGING, WILTS

Contract dated: 29 May 2003

Under the terms of the above-mentioned Contract,

I/we hereby certify that the making good of

any defects, shrinkages or other faults specified in a schedule of defects
delivered to the Contractor as an instruction

and any other defect, shrinkage or fault which has appeared within the
Defects Liability Period and has been required by an instruction to be made
good

and relating to

*Delete as
appropriate

* the Works referred to in the Certificate of Practical Completion

no. 1   dated   24 January 2003

*Section no xxxxxxxxxxxx of the Works referred to in the

Certificate of Practical Completion

no xxxxxxxxxxxx dated

*the part of the Works identified in the
Statement of Partial Possession by the Employer

no xxxxxxxxxxxx dated

was in my/our opinion completed on

23 August   20 03

To be signed by or for
the issuer named
above

Signed   *Fair & Square*

Distribution	☑ Employer	☐ Structural Engineer	☑ Planning Supervisor	☐
	☑ Contractor	☐ M&E Consultant	☐	☐
	☑ Quantity Surveyor	☑ Clerk of Works	☐	☑ File

F807A   for JCT 98

© RIBA Publications 1999

Issued by: FAIR AND SQUARE
address: 4, THE HELLOVET, CRINGING, WILTS

**Final
Certificate**

JCT 98

Employer: HUSSEIN CHARGEER
address: 1, LETSBY AVENUE, CRINGING, WILTS

Serial no: **K 101625**

Job reference: 8072

Contractor: WILLIAM DURR LTD
address: 2, THE BITTER END, CRINGING, WILTS

Date of issue: 17 September 2003

Final date for payment: 15 October 2003

Works: NEW DETACHED HOUSE
situated at: 1, LETSBY AVENUE, CRINGING, WILTS

Contract dated: 29 May 2002

Original to Employer

This Final Certificate is issued under the terms of the above-mentioned Contract.

Contract Sum adjusted as necessary . . . . £ 238,000.00

Total amount previously certified for payment to the Contractor plus amount of any advance payment . . . . £ 230,000.00

Difference between the above stated amounts . . . . £ 8,000.00

I/We hereby certify the sum of (in words)
Eight Thousand Pounds Only

All amounts are exclusive of VAT.

as a **balance due**:

* Delete as appropriate

* to the Contractor from the Employer.

x*xtoxthexEmployerxfromxthexContractorx

To be signed by or for the issuer named above

Signed *Fair & Square*

[1] Relevant only if clause 1A of the VAT Agreement applies. Delete if not applicable.

[1] The Contractor has given notice that the rate of VAT chargeable on the supply of goods and services to which the Contract relates is _____ %

[1] _____ % of the amount certified above . . . . £ _____

[1] Total of balance due and VAT amount (for information) . . . . £ _____

This is not a Tax Invoice.

F852A for JCT 98

© RIBA Publications 1999

Final Account

FINAL STATEMENT OF ACCOUNT

Employer: HUSSEIN CHARGEER

Project: 1 LETSBY AVENUE

Architect: FAIR AND SQUARE

Quantity Surveyor: ASA RULE

Ref: 8072	**Date:** 10 SEPTEMBER 2003
Contract Sum	205,000.00
LESS Contingencies	5,000.00
LESS Adjustment of PC and Provisional Sums	200,000.00
	20,000.00
ADD Adjustment of Measured Work	180,000.00
	30,500.00
ADD Contractor's Claims for Loss and/or Expense under clause 26	210,500.00
	27,500.00
	238,000.00

Contractor's Signature

W. Durt

Date: 10-9-03

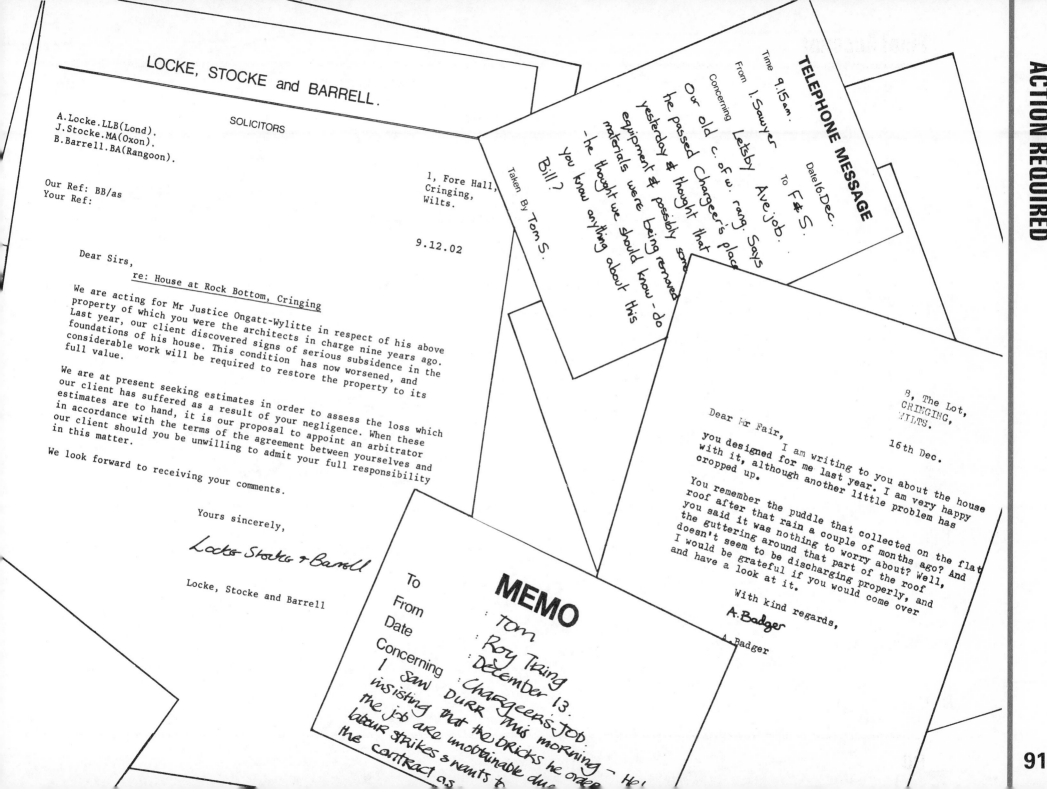

LOCKE, STOCKE and BARRELL.

SOLICITORS

A.Locke.LLB(Lond).
J.Stocke.MA(Oxon).
B.Barrell.BA(Rangoon).

Our Ref: BB/as
Your Ref:

1, Fore Hall,
Cringing,
Wilts.

9.12.02

Dear Sirs,

re: House at Rock Bottom, Cringing

We are acting for Mr Justice Ongatt-Wylitte in respect of his above property of which you were the architects in charge nine years ago. Last year, our client discovered signs of serious subsidence in the foundations of his house. This condition has now worsened, and considerable work will be required to restore the property to its full value.

We are at present seeking estimates in order to assess the loss which our client has suffered as a result of your negligence. When these estimates are to hand, it is our proposal to appoint an arbitrator in accordance with the terms of the agreement between yourselves and our client should you be unwilling to admit your full responsibility in this matter.

We look forward to receiving your comments.

Yours sincerely,

Locke Stocke & Barrell

Locke, Stocke and Barrell

TELEPHONE MESSAGE

Time 9.15am.   Date 16 Dec.

From I.Sawyer   To F & S.

Concerning Letsby Ave job. Says
Our old C. of W. rang. Says
he passed Chargeer's place
yesterday & thought that
equipment & possibly some
materials were being removed
– he thought we should know – do
you know anything about this
Bill?

Taken By Tom S.

8, The Lot,
CRINGING,
WILTS.

16th Dec.

Dear Mr Fair,
I am writing to you about the house you designed for me last year. I am very happy with it, although another little problem has cropped up.

You remember the puddle that collected on the flat roof after that rain a couple of months ago? And you said it was nothing to worry about? Well, the guttering around that part of the roof doesn't seem to be discharging properly, and I would be grateful if you would come over and have a look at it.

With kind regards,

A. Badger

A. Badger

MEMO

To   : Tom
From   : Roy Tring
Date   : December 13.
Concerning : Chargeers job.

1   Saw DURR this morning – He!
insisting that the bricks he ordered
the job are unobtainable due
labour strikes & wants to
the contract as

DESK DIARY

DEC 16

re: Letsby Ave/removal of equipment :-
I'll check this out today in person - Durr may
only be clearing up.
Materials paid for mustn't be removed, &
those on site not paid for not to be removed
without our permission.
I'll remind Durr of this if the report seems to
be accurate & inform Chargeer & see what he
wants to do. Better bone up on Determination -
just in case
      B.F.

DEC 17

re: 'unobtainable(?)' bricks.
Lets explore other alternatives (other suppliers
variation of the works etc) before we talk about
determination - it's early days yet.
In any case, Durr's contract with the supplier
seems to have been broken & he should
pursue his rights here.

DEC 18

Send to
L.S & Barrell.

Fair and Square

CHARTERED ARCHITECTS

B.FAIR.dip.arch.RIBA.
T.SQUARE.B.Arch.RIBA.AFAS.

BF/vn

4, The Hellovet,
Cringing,
Wilts.

20.12.02

Dear Mr Badger,

Thank you for your letter of the 16th December.
We are sorry to hear you still feel you have a problem with your
roof. As you know, Mr Fair visited your house on a number of
occasions since it was completed, and found nothing really to
worry about — perhaps a simple maintenance job is all that is
required.

We will of course be happy to visit you again if you wish,
and enclose a copy of the Standard Form of Agreement for
the Appointment of an Architect, together with details of
fees and expenses

We look forward to hearing from you.

Yours sincerely,

Fair & Square

Fair and Square

---

d Square

Architects

4, The Hellovet,
Cringing,
Wilts.

RE : House at Rock Bottom, Cringing.

We acknowledge receipt of your communication
dated 9.12.02 which is receiving our attention.

Bill - remember the Rock Bottom House? Trouble.
I've acknowledged L.S.B's letter & checked the files.
Our ex-partner Arthur Mild was responsible for the job
before he retired. We'd better check the partnership
agreement and inform Arthur, our insurers and
solicitors in view of the Latent Damage
Act 1986.

Tom.

SECTION EIGHT

DETERMINATION AND DISPUTE RESOLUTION

Contents

Determination

For a variety of reasons, not all contracts are fully performed. A contract can be discharged in a number of ways (see page 51), but the 1998 Standard Form makes special provision for the determination of the contractor's employment under the building contract. Of course, the common law rights of both the employer and the contractor may also be invoked.

By the employer (Clause 27)

The employer may end the contractor's employment:
- if the contractor wholly or substantially suspends the progress of the works;
- if the contractor fails to reguarly and diligently proceed with the works;
- if the contractor fails to comply with the architect's written work to be removed;
- if the contractor sub-lets or assigns a part of the work without permission as detailed in Clause 19;
- if the contractor fails to comply with CDM Regulations.

Procedure

The architect specifies the particular default to the contractor by special, recorded or actual delivery. Upon receipt of this notice, if the contractor continues the default for 14 days, the employer may determine the contractor's employment within the following 10 days or on repetition thereafter. Notice of determination must be given by special, recorded or actual delivery. If a provisional liquidator or trustee in bankruptcy is appointed or a winding up order is made, the contractor's employment is automatically determined, but it may be reinstated if the parties agree. In all other cases of insolvency, the employer may determine the contractor's employment unless the parties agree to proceed with the contract and until such time the employer need make no further payment and the contractor need do no further work. The employer does not have the right to set-off in respect of payment under any interim arrangement. The employer may take reasonable steps to protect the site, the works and any materials on site. The employer may also determine if the contractor is guilty of any corrupt act.
After determination the employer can:
- pay others to finish the work, using the contractor's equipment etc. on site;
- by written instruction of the architect, order the contractor to remove the equipment and, if not so removed within a reasonable time, sell it, holding all the proceeds (save for expenses incurred) to the contractor's credit;

- demand from the contractor payment in respect of direct loss or damage caused by the determination;
- take over the benefits of agreements with sub-contractors and suppliers, and pay them directly;
- make no further payments to the contractor until after completion and making good of defects in the works and the final cost to the employer has been established;
- opt, within 6 months of the determination, not to continue with the works and to prepare an account showing the balance owing between the parties after all the employer's expenses have been taken into account.

By the contractor (Clause 28)

The contractor may end employment:
- if the employer has not paid the sums due to the contractor within 14 days of the issuance of a certificate;
- if the employer obstructs or interferes with the issuance of a certificate;
- if the employer fails to comply with clause 19;
- if the employer fails to comply with the CDM Regulations;
- if substantially the whole works are suspended for a period named in the Appendix due to loss or damage to the works caused by:
  - late provision of information;
  - certain architect's instructions;
  - delay by the employer in work not included in the contract, or supplies undelivered;
  - if the employer fails to give access.

If the employer has not remedied the default within 14 days of receipt of notice by special, recorded or actual delivery, the contractor may determine. Furthermore, the contractor may also determine without prior notice if the employer becomes insolvent.

Procedure

The contractor should inform the employer of the determination by special, recorded or actual delivery. The contractor may then:
- remove equipment, temporary buildings etc. (taking precautions for safety);
- be paid the total retention within 28 days of the date of determination;
- claim the total value of work executed at the date of determination;
- claim direct loss or damage caused by the determination (and also loss suffered by nominated sub-contractors);

- claim costs of removal;
- claim costs of materials and goods paid for, and properly ordered in connection with the work (upon payment, they become the employer's property).

The contractor is responsible for preparing this account and the employer must pay the amount properly due within 28 days of submission with no deduction of retention.

By either party (Clause 28A)

Either party may determine the contractor's employment if substantially the whole of the uncompleted works are suspended for a continuous period named in the Appendix due to:
- force majeure;
- a specified peril;
- civil commotion;
- architect's instructions regarding discrepancies, variations or postponement due to the negligence of a local authority or statutory undertaker;
- hostilities;
- terrorist activity;

and on the expiry of the suspension period the employer or the contractor gives notice by special, recorded or actual delivery that the employment will determine within 7 days after receipt of such notice.

Procedure

The consequences are broadly the same as if the contractor determines under clause 28 except that loss or damage to the contractor or a nominated sub-contractor caused by the determination may not be claimed unless due to specified perils. The employer must prepare the account on receipt of documentation from the contractor within 2 months of the date of determination and discharge the amount within 28 days of submission to the contractor without deduction of retention.

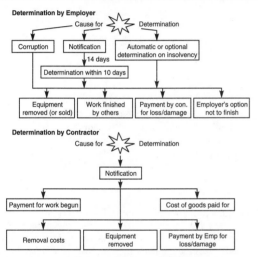

References

LAW, pp. 151–9.
THE ARCHITECT IN PRACTICE, pp. 283–7.

Dispute Resolution 1

Dispute resolution

If a dispute or difference arises between the parties to a contract, it is better if the parties can resolve the matter between themselves. However, this is not always possible and a third party may have to be called upon to settle the matter. The third party may be a civil judge or registrar should the matter be referred to the courts (see page 3). Alternatively, the dispute or difference could be referred to adjudication or arbitration. Whereas the courts are part of the English legal system and therefore subject to all its procedural and administrative elements, disputes or differences submitted to adjudication or arbitration enjoy a private and less formal process, usually in the presence of whoever the parties choose. The adjudicator or arbitrator is often someone with specific knowledge and experience in the field in which the dispute has arisen. In construction it is often an architect or surveyor who is a member of the Chartered Institute of Arbitrators, the RIBA or RICS. Like the courts, an adjudicator or arbitrator imposes a decision on the parties after considering evidence.

In recent time, the acronym ADR (Alternative Dispute Resolution) has come to the fore in the construction industry. Unfortunately, the acronym ADR is frequently used but not always clearly understood or defined. In the context it is being used, does it mean alternative to the courts, or alternative to the courts and arbitration, or something else? In this situation, it means alternative to litigation, arbitration *and* adjudication. ADR is essentially mediation or conciliation. It is not usually binding on the parties, so to be effective the parties must honestly wish to settle their differences. If they do not, they are free to pursue the matter in adjudication, arbitration or litigation. The advantages of ADR are said to be:
- saving time;
- saving money;
- promoting the continuation of cordial trading relations in the future.

ADR can take a number of forms but usually derives from one of the following:
- Conciliation or mediation. The mediator consults with both parties separately to seek common ground and areas of compromise. The mediator may be asked for conclusions or proposals which are usually non-binding.
- Mini-trial. Each side makes a short presentation of its case to a tribunal consisting of a mediator and a senior person from each side, who then retire to consider the matter. Again, the aim is to reach a settlement, although this may not always be possible.

ADR depends on the goodwill of the parties and the skill of the mediator, who should be someone who carries the respect of both parties. The function of the mediator is to help the parties reach an agreement, unlike adjudication or arbitration where a decision is imposed upon the parties. It is widely used in the USA, Australia and Hong Kong.

Arbitration

Advantages

- privacy
- convenience
- speed
- expense
- simplicity
- expertise

Privacy

Commercial secrets and reputations may be shielded from the public in a private arbitration. This would not be possible in the courts, where hearings are generally public.

Convenience

The hearing can be held anywhere to suit the parties (for example, on the site of the dispute).

Speed

Disputes can be handled quickly, without the inconvenience of having to fit into the courts' timetable. In projects where time is of the essence, this may be an important factor.

Expense

Money might be saved both in the potentially lower cost of the hearing, and in the speedy resolution of the problem.

Simplicity

Courtroom procedures may be dispensed with, according to the nature of the dispute. It is within the arbitrator's discretion to decide upon the level of informality to employ.

Expertise

Difficult construction-oriented problems may be better understood by an experienced arbitrator with knowledge in this field rather than a professional judge, e.g. an architect.

Disadvantages of arbitration

- lack of legal expertise
- precedent

Lack of legal expertise

The arbitrator, although knowledgeable in the field of the dispute, might lack a detailed understanding of the law.

Precedent

Although the arbitrator is bound to follow the precedents of caselaw, the advantage of privacy makes it inevitable that there is no collection of precedents available from completed arbitrations. This may make it difficult for a prospective party to an arbitration to assess the likelihood of success.

When to arbitrate

A matter may be referred to arbitration by:
- agreement before the dispute (possibly in the contract);
- agreement after the dispute;
- operation of law (by statute or court order).

Most construction contracts contain a provision allowing for arbitration (for example, Standard Form Article 7). Although no party can be denied access to the courts, ignoring an arbitration clause breaches the contract so that the courts, upon application, will often stay court proceedings, leaving arbitration as the sole remedy.

All arbitration agreements, as long as they are formed in writing, are governed by the Arbitration Act 1996, which provides that:

- the authority of the arbitrator can be revoked by the parties (s.23) or the arbitrator can be revoked by the courts (s.24);
- the arbitrator's award is final and binding (except for certain clearly defined situations) s.69;
- the award, if registered in the courts, will be enforceable.

This means that, although separate from the court structure, certain connections between the High Court and arbitration exist:

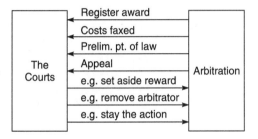

Selection

The arbitrator (or arbitrators) may be chosen:

- by agreement prior to the dispute;
- by agreement after the dispute;
- by application to a third party (the Chartered Institute of Arbitrators, perhaps, or in the case of the Standard Form, usually the President or Vice-President of the Royal Institute of British Architects).

Upon being asked to act in an arbitration, an arbitrator must assess the suitability of an arbitration to the particular dispute, and their own suitability to act. Factors preventing their acceptance of the commission would include personal knowledge of one of the parties, or an interest or bias in the matters affected.

If the arbitrator decides to act, both parties are notified. It is advisable at this stage to secure a deposit from both parties.

Directions

A benefit of arbitration is its flexibility, where the procedure can be tailored to suit the nature of the dispute. For example, the procedure could be as simple as a visit to site by the arbitrator to see the subject matter of the dispute and hear each party's case. The arbitrator then goes away to make a decision and publish an award. Alternatively, the procedure could allow for submissions by documents only or, if the dispute is of a complex nature, a hearing may be necessary. It is also possible for facets of a dispute to be dealt with by document review and partly by hearing. A meeting on site where an arbitrator inspects the work, listens to the employer and contractor present their views regarding the quality of workmanship is every bit an arbitration as when a procedure 'apes' the courts with advocates, expert witnesses and a hearing lasting 3 weeks.

Subject to any rules governing the arbitration, the arbitrator decides all procedural and evidential matters subject to the agreement of the parties. As soon as possible after the appointment, the arbitrator decides on the most appropriate procedure to resolve the dispute. To this end, the arbitrator may convene a meeting to help determine the appropriate procedure.

Prior to the actual hearing (if one is necessary), the arbitrator will direct certain preliminary matters to be undertaken by both parties so that the matter or difference in dispute is clear. Preliminary correspondence and meetings (if any) should provide for:

- statement of claim by the claimant;
- statement of defence by the respondent together with a counterclaim, if any;
- statement of defence to the counterclaim by the claimant if appropriate.

These statements should contain facts about the dispute, and may include evidence, depending on the procedure adopted. If any party is unclear as to the other's claim or defence, they may make a request for further information or clarification.

Further matters to be considered include:

- the disclosure and inspection of all documents concerned with the dispute;
- the number of experts (solicitors, barristers, expert witnesses, etc.);
- figures to be agreed as figures where possible;
- shorthand provisions. Usually the arbitrator takes notes, but with the agreement of the parties, assistance may be provided;
- whether there is to be a right of appeal from the arbitrator's decision by either party.

The hearing

The date, time and location of the hearing will be established in correspondence or at preliminary meetings. Should a party refuse to attend or be deliberately obstructive, the arbitrator, with an order from the High Court, may commence with the proceeding EX PARTE (that is, in the party's absence), provided that the absentee has been informed of the right to attend.

The procedure of the hearing is likely to follow that of a court of law, abiding by the rules of evidence, although the arbitrator has wide powers to conduct the hearing depending upon the circumstances and the wishes of the parties.

JCT Arbitration Rules 1998

JCT forms of contract provide for arbitration to be carried out under the JCT Construction Industry Model Arbitration Rules 1998. They include three procedures for the conduct of the arbitration:

- Rule 8 Documents only;
- Rule 7 Short hearing;
- Rule 9 Full procedure.

Under Rule 6 the arbitrator, as soon as is appropriate, must consider the appropriate form of procedure given the dispute. To this end, the parties provide the arbitrator and the other party with details of the dispute, need for and length of hearing, and proposals for the appropriate procedure for the dispute, i.e. Rules 7, 8 or 9. After a procedural meeting, the arbitrator gives appropriate directions on the procedure to be adopted.

The powers held by the arbitrator include:

- the taking of legal advice;
- giving directions for protecting, storing or disposing of property which is the subject matter of the dispute;
- ordering a party to give security of costs;
- proceeding in the absence of a party after appropriate notice;
- directing that costs are to be determined by the arbitrator;
- directing that evidence be given by affidavit;
- ordering any party to the dispute supply copies of documents which the arbitrator decides are relevant.

Costs and the award

Throughout the arbitration, the arbitrator must apply the law. Arbitrators are bound to follow past decisions of the courts in deciding the matters before them unless the parties agree otherwise.

After receiving or hearing the parties' cases, the arbitrator must, within a reasonable time, make an award. The parties are free to agree the form of the award. If there is no agreement, the award shall be in writing, setting out the arbitrator's reasons and signed and dated by the arbitrator or arbitrators. Reasons need not be given if it is an award embodying an agreement by the parties or the parties agree to dispense with reasons. The award should state the seat of the award e.g. England, France. Notification that the award is complete is then given to both parties. Either may take up the award, but usually must pay the arbitrator's fees before doing so. If the collecting party has won its case, the losing party will usually reimburse the arbitrator's fee, as costs generally follow the event.

Appeal and points of law

Under s.1 of the 1996 Act the courts do not intervene with the process unless provided for within the Act. Unless the parties otherwise agree, a party may appeal on a point of law arising out of an award, on a matter of the arbitrator's jurisdiction (though this right can be lost) or on a serious irregularity arising from the proceedings. However, both parties can, in writing, agree to exclude the right to appeal, thus making the award truly final and binding, provided that such an agreement is made after the arbitration has commenced.

Unless otherwise agreed by the parties, the court may hear an application from a party to determine a PRELIMINARY POINT OF LAW if either the tribunal or the parties to the reference agree. The court must be satisfied that substantial cost savings will be made, and that the application was made without delay.

The expert witness

It is possible that an architect may be called to an arbitration to give an expert opinion regarding matters concerning a building dispute. Whereas the ordinary witness gives evidence of the facts as observed, the expert witness gives an opinion based upon those facts. Expert witnesses are not usually connected with the case before the dispute, and are called by one of the parties because their evidence supports a particular case.

It is usual for each party to provide their own expert witness (or witnesses), and to pay the appropriate fees involved in their employment. Although opinions given by expert witnesses on opposing sides of a dispute are likely to differ, they must be made in good faith and be sincerely held. It is the expert's duty to assist the arbitrator to arrive at the truth.

If the parties agree, they can appoint a single joint expert.

The architect as arbitrator

Professional qualification and experience in the field of architecture suggests an expertise in the construction field which may provide a foundation for arbitration work. The Chartered Institute of Arbitrators runs a number of courses and examinations for prospective members who wish to apply for Associateship, Membership or Fellowship status.

Further information may be obtained from:
THE CHARTERED INSTITUTE OF ARBITRATORS
International Arbitration and Mediation Centre
12 Bloomsbury Square
London
WC1A 2LP

References

LAW, pp. 62–3.
ARCHITECT'S LEGAL HANDBOOK, pp. 178–90.

Adjudication

A statutory right to adjudication was introduced by the Housing Grants, Construction and Regeneration Act 1996 for the parties to a *'construction contract'* (see page 52). Section 108 of the Act states that every *'construction contract'* shall:

- enable a party to give a notice of intention to refer a difference or dispute to adjudication;
- provide a timetable to allow an adjudicator to be appointed and the dispute to be referred to that person, both within seven days;
- enable the adjudicator to reach a decision within 28 days of the dispute or difference being referred. The parties by agreement may give the adjudicator additional time. However, with the agreement of the referring party, the adjudicator may be granted an additional 14 days in which to make a decision;

| Notice of intention to refer dispute | 7 days | Appoint adjudicator & refer dispute | 28 days | Adjudicator reach decison | 14 days | Extend period for adjudicator to reach decision agreed by referring party |

- impose a duty on the adjudicator to act impartially;
- enable the adjudicator to take the initiative in ascertaining the facts and the law.

If a contract does not comply with s.108, the provisions within the Scheme for Construction Contracts (England and Wales) Regulation 1998 will apply to the contract. In effect, if the contract entered into fails to set out a procedure complying with s.108, the Scheme will apply to the parties as if it were part of their contract. Most, if not all, of the standard forms have been amended to comply with the provisions of the Act.

The Scheme

The Scheme sets out the requirements with regard to the Notice of Intention to seek adjudication, the appointment of an adjudicator, the powers of an adjudicator, the decision and the effect of the decision.

A Notice of Intention to refer a difference or dispute to adjudication should include the following:

- the names and addresses of the parties to the contract;
- the nature and a brief description of the dispute;
- details of where and when the dispute arose;
- the redress sought.

The parties could name the adjudicator in their contract, or are free to agree on who the adjudicator is to be. If no agreement can be reached, the referring party would seek the appointment by a nominating body. A nominating body is one that publicly holds itself out as an entity who would appoint an adjudicator if asked to do so by a referring party, e.g. RIBA or RICS. The nominating body has to make the appointment within 5 working days of receiving a request.

An adjudicator's authority may be revoked at any time by agreement of the parties, and an adjudicator may resign upon written notice to the parties. In such an instance, the referring party would serve a fresh Notice and seek the appointment of another adjudicator. An adjudicator must resign the appointment if the dispute is the same or substantially the same as one previously referred to adjudication. A dispute can only be adjudicated upon once. A party who does not wish to accept the decision of an adjudicator must refer the dispute to arbitration or litigation, where the whole dispute would be heard again – it is not an appeal from the adjudicator's decision. In the meantime, a party must abide by the adjudicator's decision.

An adjudicator is duty bound to act impartially in carrying out duties and, unless owing to a lack of good faith, is not liable for anything done or omitted in the discharge of such duties. In fact, the courts have held that even if an adjudicator gets the facts or the law wrong, they will still uphold the decision.

Under the Scheme, an adjudicator is given wide powers concerning the conduct of the adjudication. The adjudicator can take the initiative in ascertaining both the facts and law which includes:

- requesting a party (or parties) to supply documentation or written submissions;
- meeting the parties and asking questions of the parties or their representatives;
- having tests carried out on the subject matter of the dispute.

The decision of an adjudicator is binding upon the parties, who must comply with the decision until the dispute is finally determined by arbitration or litigation. If one of the parties so requests, the adjudicator shall give reasons for the decision, though such an approach will obviously involve more time for an adjudicator and thereby increase their fees.

An adjudicator is entitled to charge fees reasonably incurred, with both parties being jointly and severally liable for such fees. The adjudicator's decision will usually determine who is to bear the cost of the fees, and unless the parties have agreed otherwise, it is normal that the parties will carry the burden of their own costs in the adjudication.

JCT Standard Form of Contract 1998

Rather than rely on the provisions of the Scheme, most standard forms have been amended by their relative drafting bodies to comply with s.108. Article 5 and Condition 41A in the Standard Form.

The adjudicator is a person either agreed by the parties or appointed by the nominating body identified in the Appendix. The RIBA are the default nominating body. Once appointed, the parties are required to execute with the adjudicator the JCT Adjudication Agreement. This is a simple agreement that addresses the adjudicator's fees, obligations and termination of the Agreement.

The referring part is to refer the difference or dispute to the appointed adjudicator within 7 days of the Notice to refer. If the adjudicator is not appointed within 7 days, the referral is made immediately upon the appointment being made. A copy of the referral document should be served at the same time on the other party as on the adjudicator. It is possible to serve the referral document by fax, but this must be backed up with a copy by either first class post or actual delivery. The adjudicator must confirm actual receipt of the referral document. Within 7 days of the date of the referral, the responding party must submit a response referred to as *'a written statement of the contentions upon which it relies'*.

Within 28 days of the referral, the adjudicator must give a decision unless the period is extended by the agreement of the parties, or by up to 14 days with the agreement of the referring party.

In conducting the adjudication, the adjudicator is given wide powers, e.g. obtaining information, requiring the parties to undertake tests on the disputed matter, visiting the site and using personal knowledge and experience.

The adjudicator is not obliged to give reasons for a decision.

Each party shall meet its own costs, but the adjudicator may direct which of the parties, or possibly both equally, is to carry the costs of any tests or the opening up of the works. The adjudicator in the decision is to state which of the parties is to pay the adjudictor's costs and, if the decision is silent on the matter, each party bears the costs in equal proportions.

Useful Addresses

ARCHITECT'S REGISTRATION BOARD
8 Weymouth Street
London W1W 5BU
(www.arb.org.uk)

ARCHITECTURE AND SURVEYING INSTITUTE
St Mary House
15 St Mary Street
Chippenham
Wilts SN15 3JN
(www.asi.org.uk)

THE ASSOCIATION OF CONSULTANT ARCHITECTS
LIMITED
98 Hayes Road
Bromley
Kent BR2 9AB
(www.acarchitects.co.uk)

BARBOUR INDEX LIMITED
New Lodge
Drift Road
Windsor
Berks SL4 4RQ
(www.barbourexpert.com)

BRITISH INSTITUTE OF ARCHITECTURAL
TECHNOLOGISTS
397 City Road
London EC1V 1NH
(www.BIAT.org.uk)

BUILDING CENTRE
26 Store Street
London WC1E 7BT
(www.buildingcentre.co.uk)

BUILDING RESEARCH ESTABLISHMENT LIMITED
Bucknalls Lane
Garston
Watford WD25 9XX
(www.bre.co.uk)

CHARTERED INSTITUTE OF ARBITRATORS
12 Bloomsbury Square
London WC1A 2LP
(www.arbitrators.org.uk)

CONSTRUCTION CONFEDERATION
Construction House
56–64 Leonard Street
London EC2A 4JX
(www.constructionconfederation.co.uk)

CONSTRUCTION INDUSTRY COMPUTING ASSOCIATION
1 Trust Court
Histon
Cambridge CB2 3QQ
(www.cica.org.uk)

CONSTRUCTION INDUSTRY COUNCIL
26 Store Street
London WC1E 7BT
(www.cic.org.uk)

CONSTRUCTION INDUSTRY RESEARCH AND
INFORMATION ASSOCIATION
6 Storey's Gate
London SW1P 3AU
(www.ciria.org.uk)

GOVERNMENT BOOKSHOPS
The Stationery Office
St Clement's House
2–16 Colegate
Norwich NR3 1BQ
(www.hmso.gov.uk)

INSTITUTE OF CLERKS OF WORKS OF GREAT BRITAIN
INCORPORATED
41 The Mall
Ealing
London W5 3TJ
(www.icwgb.sagehost.co.uk)

INSTITUTION OF CIVIL ENGINEERS
1 Great George Street
London SW1P 3AA
(www.ice.org.uk)

LANDSCAPE INSTITUTE
6–8 Barnard Mews
London SW11 1QU
(www.l-i.org.uk)

NBS SERVICES
The Old Post Office
St Nicholas Street
Newcastle-upon-Tyne NE1 1RH
(www.nbsservices.co.uk)

ROYAL INCORPORATION OF ARCHITECTS IN SCOTLAND
15 Rutland Square
Edinburgh EH1 2BE
(www.rias.org.uk)

ROYAL INSTITUTE OF BRITISH ARCHITECTS
66 Portland Place
London W1B 1AD
(www.architecture.com)

ROYAL INSTITUTION OF CHARTERED SURVEYORS
12 Great George Street
Parliament Square
London SW1P 3AD
(www.rics.org.uk)

ROYAL SOCIETY OF ULSTER ARCHITECTS
2 Mount Charles
Belfast BT7 1NZ
(www.rsua.org.uk)

ROYAL TOWN PLANNING INSTITUTE
41 Botolph Lane
London EC3R 8DL
(www.rtpi.org.uk)

PLANNING
To obtain planning appeal forms and information regarding procedure write to:

IN ENGLAND
The Planning Inspectorate
Customer Support Unit
Room 3/15 Eagle Wing
Temple Quay House
2 The Square
Temple Quay
Bristol BS1 6PN

IN WALES
The Planning Inspectorate
Room 1-004
Cathays Park
Cardiff CF10 3NQ

IN NORTHERN IRELAND
Planning Appeals Commission
Park House
87–91 Great Victoria Street
Belfast BT2 7AG

IN SCOTLAND
Scottish Executive
Victoria Quay
Edinburgh EH6 6QQ

If it is believed that the appeal procedure is not satisfactorily adhered to, details should be sent to:

The Council on Tribunals
22 Kingsway
London WC2B 6LE

Bibliography

Select bibliography

These books have been used as reference sources throughout the text:

BARKER, David and PADFIELD, Colin
LAW
10th Edition, 1998
MADE SIMPLE, OXFORD

CHAPPELL, David and WILLIS, Andrew
THE ARCHITECT IN PRACTICE
8th Edition, 2000
BLACKWELL SCIENCE, OXFORD

COX, Stanley and HAMILTON, Alaine (Editors)
ARCHITECT'S HANDBOOK OF PRACTICE MANAGEMENT
6th Edition, 1998
RIBA PUBLICATIONS, LONDON

GREEN, Ronald
THE ARCHITECT'S GUIDE TO RUNNING A JOB
6th Edition, 2001
ARCHITECTURAL PRESS, OXFORD

SPEAIGHT, Anthony and STONE, Gregory (Editors)
ARCHITECT'S LEGAL HANDBOOK
7th Edition, 2000
ARCHITECTURAL PRESS, OXFORD

STEPHENSON, John
BUILDING REGULATIONS EXPLAINED: 2000 REVISION
6th Edition, 2001
SPON PRESS, LONDON

Further Reading

Further reading

These books are recommended for reference where a more extensive coverage of a subject area is required:

CARNELL, Nicholas
CAUSATION AND DELAY
2000
BLACKWELL SCIENCE, OXFORD

CECIL, Ray
PROFESSIONAL LIABILITY
3rd Edition, 1991
LEGAL STUDIES AND SERVICES (PUBLISHING)

CHAPPELL, David
PARRIS'S STANDARD FORM OF CONTRACT
3rd Edition, 2002
BLACKWELL PUBLISHING, OXFORD

CHAPPELL, David
STANDARD LETTERS IN ARCHITECTURAL PRACTICE
3rd Edition, 2002
BLACKWELL PUBLISHING, OXFORD

CHAPPELL, David, MARSHALL, Derek, POWELL-SMITH, Vincent and CAVENDER, Simon
BUILDING CONTRACT DICTIONARY
3rd Edition, 2001
BLACKWELL SCIENCE, OXFORD

CRESSWELL, H. B.
THE HONEYWOOD FILE & THE HONEYWOOD SETTLEMENT
1929–1930, Reprinted 1983
ARCHITECTURAL PRESS, OXFORD

EMMITT, Stephen and YEOMANS, David
SPECIFYING BUILDINGS
2001
BUTTERWORTH-HEINEMANN, OXFORD

FURST, Stephen and RAMSEY, Vivian
KEATING ON BUILDING CONTRACTS
7th Edition, 2001
SWEET & MAXWELL, LONDON

HEAP, Desmond
AN OUTLINE OF PLANNING LAW
11th Edition, 1996
SWEET & MAXWELL, LONDON

HICKLING, A. and FRIEND, J.
PLANNING UNDER PRESSURE 1997
ARCHITECTURAL PRESS, OXFORD

HYAMS, David
CONSTRUCTION COMPANION TO BRIEFING
2001
RIBA ENTERPRISES

LUPTON, Sarah (Editor)
ARCHITECT'S JOB BOOK
7th Edition, 2000
RIBA PUBLICATIONS, LONDON

REISS, Geoff
PROJECT MANAGEMENT DEMYSTIFIED
2nd Edition, 1996
SPON PRESS, LONDON

SPEDDING, A.
CIOB HANDBOOK OF FACILITIES MANAGEMENT
1994
LONGMAN, LONDON

UFF, John
CONSTRUCTION LAW
7th Edition, 1999
SWEET & MAXWELL, LONDON

WALLACE, Duncan
HUDSON'S BUILDING AND ENGINEERING CONTRACTS
11th Edition, 1990
SWEET & MAXWELL, LONDON

RIBA Publications

Other useful RIBA Publications include:

Architect's Guide to Adjudication
Architect's Guide to Arbitration
The Architect in Dispute Resolution
Party Walls Workbook
Architect's Guide to Job Administration under the CDM Regulations 1994
Code of Professional Conduct
Clerk of Works Manual
Starting Up in Practice
Group Practice and Consortia

NJCC Publications

Code of Procedure for Single Stage Selective Tendering, 1996
Code of Procedure for Two Stage Selective Tendering, 1996
Code of Procedure for Selective Tendering for Design and Build 1996

Cases

Statutes

Glossary

Glossary of common legal terms

Ab initio	from the beginning
Bona fide	in good faith
Caveat emptor	let the buyer beware
Ejusdem generis	of the same type
Estoppel	a rule of evidence which prevents a person from denying or asserting a fact owing to a previous act
Ex parte	upon the application of
Ignorantis juris non excusat	ignorance of the law is no excuse
In personam	against a person i.e. not against everyone
In rem	against a thing i.e. applicable to everyone
Inter se	amongst themselves
Obiter dicta	things said by the way
Per se	by itself
Prima facie	on first view
Quantum meruit	as much as he deserves
Ratio decidendi	reason for the decision
Res ipsa loquitur	the thing speaks for itself
Stare decisis	to stand by past decisions
Sui juris	of legal capacity
Tortfeasor	one liable for a civil wrong, except re. contract or trust matters
Uberrimae fidei	of the utmost good faith
Ultra vires	beyond one's powers
Volenti non fit injuria	no wrong can be done to one who consents to the action

Index

Index